TABOR EVANS

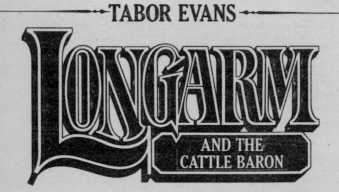

AND THE CATTLE BARON

A JOVE BOOK

LONGARM AND THE CATTLE BARON

A Jove Book / published by arrangement with
the author

PRINTING HISTORY
Jove edition / April 1984

ISBN: 0-515-06265-0

Jove books are published by The Berkley Publishing Group,
200 Madison Avenue, New York, N.Y. 10016. The words
"A JOVE BOOK" and the "J" with sunburst are trademarks
belonging to Jove Publications, Inc.

PRINTED IN THE UNITED STATES OF AMERICA

LONGARM

AND THE
CATTLE BARON

Chapter 1

The dozen tired and dusty riders were tracking the Kiowa Kid against the prevailing prairie winds from the west. When some of their mounts began to act up, the sheriff who was leading them reined in, waved his Winchester for attention, and called out, "Hold her right here, gents! Something on the windward side of that rise ahead is spooking our ponies. We'd best move in on it dismountful."

The determined but cautious old lawman had chosen his *posse comitatus* with some care. All but two of them had ridden with him before. So those two got to mind the mounts as the others trailed the sheriff up the slope ahead on foot.

Halfway up the grassy rise the sheriff pointed out a break in the sun-bleached sod with his saddle gun's muzzle and remarked to his nearest deputy, "He's still riding that over-sized hoss he stole from them nesters, the dumb bastard."

Then the sheriff sniffed, grimaced, and added thoughtfully, "Mister Death has rid this way recent, too. For I smells his sickening sweet breath on the soft summer breeze. Cover me. I'm going over."

Suiting his actions to his words, the old lawman forged on up the slope in a running crouch, levering a Winchester round in its chamber as he neared the crest. But when he

1

topped the rise he stopped, stood tall, and stared morosely down into the draw on the far side for a time. Finally he turned to call back, "Show's over, gents. We've caught up with the Kiowa Kid at last. But it seems the muley son of a bitch has gone and got his fool self kilt!"

The others followed as the saddle-sore old lawman moved down for a closer look at the messy remains of a slender youth who'd died dressed Buscadero-Brag in a dusty black outfit trimmed with tarnished German silver. The cadaver sprawled facedown across a yards-wide colony of red bulldog ants. The ants were feeding on their unexpected guest. But though their vicious little jaws more than lived up to their red-pepper complexions, it seemed more likely that the immediate cause of death had been that arrow in the ant-covered body's back.

The arrow had gone in deep. The shaft rising from between the dead youth's shoulder blades was fletched with owl feathers and striped with vermilion medicine paint.

The body was missing its hat, boots and guns. The head had been scalped—a lot. The skull was exposed from the nape of the neck up. One of the men asked the sheriff if he didn't agree the Kiowa Kid had likely met up with Sioux.

The sheriff lit a smoke to gather his thoughts before he replied. "It sure don't look like a suicide," he said. "That arrow's Hunkpapa Teton Sioux or I'll eat it raw. But we surely have us a perplexful constitutional question here, gents."

Another posse rider who'd circled for sign before joining the group standing over the corpse spat and said, "The same rainy spell as made it so easy to track this cuss tells a tale of two critters lighting out to the south, Sheriff. One was that big draft hoss the kid was riding. The other was an unshod Injun pony. It ain't hard to read what must have happened hereabouts. The Kiowa Kid was riding desperate.

For he'd never planned on that unseasonable rain when he kilt that nester, raped his woman, and lit out on a fresh mount with such unusual feet. He must have knowed a schoolmarm could track him across soft ground no matter which way he rode across Dakota Territory. So he was considering his past instead of his future when he met up with Sioux and—"

"Dang it, Ike," the sheriff cut in, "I don't need you to tell me how this murderous son of a bitch got kilt! The part as has me confused is what in thunder I'm supposed to *do* about it! It can't be constitutional for some fool Sioux to be off the reservation killing white folks. But on the other hand, this dead rascal was wanted dead or alive and I disremember any small print saying just who was or who was not allowed to kill him."

Ike stared down thoughtfully and observed, "Far be it from me to say this mad-dog killer didn't have a killing coming, Sheriff. But I don't hold with sassy Sioux lifting *any* white man's hoss and hair! So what say we just track down the buck as counted coup on the Kiowa Kid and teach him some proper respect for his superiors?"

There was a growl of agreement, but the sheriff shook his head. "Simmer down, gents. In the first damned place, said Sioux has at least a good two days' lead on us, judging from the smell of this mess he left for us to clean up. If we *could* catch up, we might well find a dozen of us facing Lord knows how many of them, off the reservation to do Lord knows what. I rid against the Hunkpapa Teton Sioux back in Seventy-six, and I can tell you all from painful personal experience, it's a chore best left to the U. S. Cavalry."

He took a deep drag on his smoke before he added wearily, "In the *second* damned place, the infernal Indian agency might raise a stink if we was to shoot us an Injun for the

3

killing of fair game. This here dead meat belonged to an outlaw wanted dead or alive, remember?"

Another deputy dropped to one knee beside the corpse and put a hand on it. "That can't be right, Sheriff!" he protested. "This old boy wasn't took dead or alive. He was massacred by wild Indians!"

Then he yelped like a kicked hound and sprang back to his feet to beat at his jeans with desperation as well as his Stetson. The others laughed and the ant just went on biting him.

The sheriff laughed, too, then said, "Any man with a lick of sense wouldn't have to get his fool self et alive by ants to figure any Injun robbing a dead man of his boots and guns would hardly leave anything worth mention in his damned old pockets, Jim."

He took another drag on his smoke. "Don't nobody else trifle with this body, neither," he went on. "We'll ride back to town the short way to fetch the undertaker and that newspaper gent as owns the box camera. I wants a photograph of what we found here, just the way we found it, afore I turns the case over to the federal government."

Ike, the would-be Indian fighter, asked what in thunder the federal government had to do with the death of a rascal wanted in Dakota Territory.

The sheriff explained, "The Kiowa Kid was wanted lots of places. Some of the papers out on him was federal. And before anyone gets his bowels in an uproar, I told you all when I deputized you that no Dakota bounties was posted on the son of a bitch just for killing and raping nester folks. So there's no profit worth mention in us fretting ourselves further about the killing of a federal want on federal open range by a ward or wards of the federal government."

Ike still looked unconvinced, but an older and wiser, or perhaps just more trail-weary deputy laughed. "Hot damn,

4

I follows your drift, Sheriff," he said. "I votes we just turn this bucket of snakes over to our dear old Uncle Sam and let *him* figure it out!"

Uncle Sam and his nephews in Washington were just as confused, or more so, as other snakes kept getting added to the bucket. The poor soul stuck with it on his desk for the moment sat sweating in his hot, stuffy office, reading another telegram from the Bureau of Indian Affairs, when an aide came in, sank wearily into the chair on the junior side of the desk, and complained, "Those bastards in Interior insist that killing on their own goddamned open range is a Justice case. I just came from State and *those* bastards tell me they can't do a damned thing about that other gripe from Dakota Territory, either!"

The man behind the desk waved another telegram. "The War Department says *they* can't move without verification that hostiles are off the reservation in force. According to this wire from the Indian Agent at Standing Rock, not a creature was stirring, not even a mouse, when somebody put a Hunkpapa Teton arrow in that outlaw out there. All of White Bull's braves were tucked in their reservation beds with visions of sugarplums dancing through their heads, it says here."

His aide grimaced. "Maybe red man speak with forked tongue," he said. "Or maybe the mysterious buck rode up from Pine Ridge, or, better yet, Rosebud Reservation. That photograph showed a lad scalped more Cheyenne than Sioux, you know."

"Spare me Indian lore," his boss said. "*They* don't read it, either. Pine Ridge and Rosebud both report all their wards present and accounted for as well. Meanwhile, since no other whites have been menaced by Indians on or off the reservation for a while, I think we can safely leave the

5

mysterious death of the Kiowa Kid on the back of the stove for now. What was that other gripe from the territorial government out there? It's so damned hot I can barely remember my own name!"

The aide wiped his own sweaty face and replied, "His Highness, Prince Deltorsky, is at it again. Those fools in Land Management must have been crazy, drunk, bribed, or all three when they granted a homestead claim to a god-damned Russian prince!"

He caught the warning look from his superior and quickly added, "All right, I won't say anyone was *bribed*. But it was still mighty stupid. Prince Deltorsky pays no attention to territorial or any other kind of American law. He claims that as a subject of the Czar he doesn't have to. He's set up what he calls a ranch, but what's more accurately described as a robber barony. He's got his own private army of cossack retainers and when he wants someone else's water, range, or, some say, woman, lots of luck!"

The man behind the desk rummaged through a drawer. "It's coming back to me now," he muttered. "Didn't one of his cossacks trifle with some woman in . . . What's the name of that little town out there? I can't find the damned complaint."

"Middle Fork, sir. The sheriff there is the same lawman who found that Kiowa Kid dead and scalped on the prairie west of town. He had even less luck trying to serve a warrant for molestation on one of Prince Deltorsky's ruffians the other day. The prince evoked diplomatic immunity and threatened to sic his dogs on the sheriff. Said sheriff said that when a man out that way doesn't act like a tidy neighbor, he might find himself entertaining a vigilance committee some evening, diplomatic or not. The territorial governor is the one who filed the official complaint. Says he's worried he won't be able to control the situation much longer unless somebody or something gives."

6

The man behind the desk made a tent with his fingers as he leaned back in his swivel chair and mused aloud. "I didn't know diplomatic immunity extended down to rough-hewn hired help."

His aide said, "It shouldn't, sir. But apparently State thinks it does. I don't see why we in the Justice Department have to worry about the case at all, since we can't do a thing about the prince and his uncouth cossacks with our hands tied by diplomacy in high places."

He unfastened his tie and opened his collar. "Besides," he added, "if I know the Dakotas, the arrogant bastard is riding for a fall without our help! He doesn't have *all* the hardcased riders out that way in his private army, you know. So why can't we just wait until the inevitable vigilantes burn him out and then just move in on *them?* We're allowed to arrest our *own* night riders, right?"

"We are indeed. But it's too sloppy. Our job is to keep the peace, not to create international incidents. But your mention of vigilantes had jogged my memory and I sense a picture emerging from the mists. Doesn't Marshal Billy Vail in the Denver office have a deputy who's dealt with vigilantes indeed?"

The aide grimaced and said, "Oh, you must mean that disciplinary problem, Deputy Custis Long. They call him Longarm. He's said to be a pretty good lawman, but he's far too wild to consider putting on a case involving *diplomacy,* for God's sake!"

His superior grinned like a mean little kid. "Right, it's all coming back to me now. Longarm's worked more than once with the B.I.A., and I understand he's one of the few white men the Sioux respect and trust. I think we'll just ask Billy Vail to send him up to Standing Rock to have a powwow with old White Bull."

The aide nodded and said, "Longarm ought to be able to get White Bull to talk, if any white man can. Who do we saddle with the gripes about Prince Deltorsky and his cossacks?"

"Who in the Devil *could* we send after a big shot with diplomatic immunity? Just have Vail aim Longarm up that way and—ah—we shall see what we shall see."

The aide caught on and grinned like another mean little kid. "Naturally we don't mention Prince Deltorsky to Marshal Vail at all, sir?"

"Good God, no! Old Billy Vail has survived too many departmental head-rolling contests to risk his job by sending a ruffian like Longarm on a mission calling for the utmost delicacy and tact. He'd select some deputy who *understood* diplomatic immunity, the poor simp would understand there was nothing he could do about our resident robber baron, and *then* where would we be?"

"You mean you just want to shove a bull into a diplomatic china shop, blindfolded, sir?"

The man behind the desk looked pained. He shook his head and said, "I mean that my old friend Billy Vail will be sending a disciplinary problem with a rough sense of justice to investigate a case having not a thing to do with His pain-in-the-ass Highness, Prince Deltorsky. If I know Longarm's record, once some fair damsel tells him she's been pinched on her little bottom by a cossack, he won't *give* a damn about diplomatic immunity, and nobody from this office will have any further control over the results. So, look—no matter how things turn out when the smoke settles, your ass will be covered, my ass will be covered, and, hell, for all we know, Marshal Vail's ass will be covered!"

"What about Longarm's ass, sir?"

"What do you want, egg in your beer? It's not your ass, or mine!"

Chapter 2

At about the time the Western Union night letter from Washington was arriving in Denver, the object of its tender concern was having a diplomatic problem of his own. Longarm had just woken up in a strange bed with a stange woman whose name he just couldn't recall.

Whoever she was, she seemed friendly as hell, and she wasn't bad looking, if you didn't mind redheads with black roots to their hair. The beauty mark on her cheek was a fake, too, as she gazed fondly down at him, screwing on top.

He grinned back up at her, cupping her generous pale breasts in his suntanned hands lest she hurt them with all that bouncing as she rode his shaft like a kid on a merry-go-round. "Oh, Custis, I can feel you getting harder inside me," she said. He just went on grinning, wondering who in thunder she was.

It only stood to reason he'd be rising more to the occasion now that he was wide awake. It had surely felt odd waking up with it in her at half-mast, not remembering ever putting it in her in the first damned place. But whoever she was, she sure bounced pretty, and in next to no time at all he'd fired his sunrise salute up into her and, judging from the way she collapsed all weak down against his naked chest, she'd come, too.

She rolled half off and nuzzled his neck with her moist lips as she toyed with his virility, or what was left of it, with her free hand, crooning, "Oh, Custis, you're so masterful. You know how hard I tried to defend my honor, but when a woman tries her best, and in trying, fails, it's the same as if she succeeded, isn't it?"

"If you say so, little darling," he replied, trying to figure out where in hell he was.

It was slowly coming back to him that some time in the recent past he'd been coming back to Denver aboard the Burlington Flyer and, right, he'd been drinking in the club car, and, yeah, there *had* been a sort of shy-looking redhead drinking alone at a table in a corner. He propped himself up on one elbow for a better view of his surroundings and, well, this *could* be the same gal, give or take the duds she'd been wearing on the train. She looked less shy, naked as a jay beside him on the rumpled linens. So he rolled aboard her to renew their acquaintance.

She opened her lush creamy thighs in welcome, of course, but as he entered her again, and even as she wrapped her arms and legs around him to respond to his movements, she went on talking dumb.

She sobbed, "Oh, Lord knows I'm *trying* to be virtuous, but what's a poor woman to do when a man's so persistent?"

"Uh, you want me to stop, ma'am?"

"No, now that the damage has been done, there's no use resisting your passion. Could you move a little faster, dear?"

That sounded fair. So he just shut up and kept pounding until they'd both climaxed again. He stayed in the saddle, letting it soak, as he wondered what time it was. The pale gray light through the lace curtains said it was morning, and if he'd been on that infernal train on a Tuesday night, this had to be Wednesday, and a *work* day, damn it!

He started moving again, knowing it would be impolite to quit this soon, but that he'd be in for a tedious chewing at the office if he took much longer saying adios polite.

"Can you really do it again so soon?" she marveled.

He said, "Well, it'd go faster, dog style. And we do have to study on getting up to go to work. You did say you had a job, didn't you?"

"Silly, don't you remember my telling you I was a wait-ress? I do have to be at the Café by eight-thirty. What was that you mentioned about some other style being quicker?"

So he dismounted and proceeded to show her how to do it dog style. She let him position her right, but sobbed, "Oh, no, it's so...so *undignified* on my hands and knees like this!"

But he was getting used to the funny way she talked, now, and sure enough, as he entered her from the rear, standing with his bare feet on the rug, she arched her spine to take it deep and proceeded to wag her butt like a happy pup even as she protested, "I'll never be able to look you in the face again!"

He smiled fondly down at her. She giggled and told him he was just awful. "My Heavens, it feels so *conversational*, facing away from you like this. Do you mind if I ask you a question, dear?"

"Go ahead, honey."

"How on earth did you *do* it? I mean, I had no intention of letting anyone on that train even *speak* to me! When you came over to join me I distinctly remember making a firm resolve to resist your advances to the death. And then, the next thing I knew, you'd somehow gotten me to this funny little hotel and—I can't believe it! I'm coming *again!*"

That made two of them. He closed his eyes and pounded his way to glory as she sobbed and chewed the sheets, enjoying a repeated or protracted orgasm until she finally fell off to lie facedown across the bed, protesting that she wasn't the kind of girl he must be taking her for.

He stepped over to the washstand, cleaned up, and gathered his duds from the floor where they were scattered with her. Then he sat on the edge of the bed to commence dressing.

She propped herself up to watch, wistfully, as he soothed, "We'll talk about it later, after we both get off this evening."

"You still want me, now that I'm a fallen woman?"

He didn't answer. In the first place, that was a mighty dumb question. In the second, he wasn't sure of the answer. The red-headed waitress gal was pretty, and she screwed just fine, but what in thunder would they ever *talk* about, between times?

In the end, of course, he assured her of his undying love and affection as they kissed adios, her still naked, with his gun rig likely discomforting against her bare belly. It wasn't until he was out on the sandstone sidewalk, trying to get his bearings in the cold gray morning light of somewhere in Denver, that Longarm realized he still didn't know the redhead's name, where she worked, or how in thunder he meant to look her up after work or, for that matter, ever again.

He turned to gaze thoughtfully up at the front of the seedy little no-questions-asked hotel he'd just left. He knew where he was now, for he'd spent other nights back there with other sudden friends.

He fished out a cheroot as he pondered going back to ask some likely awkward questions. Then he lit the smoke, turned away, and headed for the office in the federal building. He didn't want to be late for work, he had some ground to cover, and there were times when it just made more sense for a man to quit while he was ahead.

Longarm hadn't reported for work so early in recent memory. But his boss, Marshal William Vail, saw no need to praise his deputy for showing up just as Vail was unlocking the office door. The shorter, older, and plumper lawman frowned up at the taller, younger, whipcord-muscular Longarm to ask laconically, "What happened? Did her husband walk in on you?"

Longarm didn't answer. The coffee he'd washed a hasty breakfast down with on the way over hadn't had time to wake him up yet.

Vail opened the door. "Well, don't just stand in the infernal hall all day on the taxpayers' time, damn it," he said. "Let's go on back to my inner sanctum. I got some shit for you to shovel. Some of it come in yesterday whilst you was taking your own sweet time getting back from that field job I know damn well you wrapped up two days ago. A night letter from Washington was delivered to my house this morning just in time to spoil my breakfast."

Longarm followed his superior back to the oak-paneled private office, wondering why old Billy was so broody. His boss had never been noted for having a sunny disposition before lunch, but Longarm sensed he was pissed beyond the usual requirements of his position this morning.

Vail waved Longarm to a seat in the usual leather-covered chair by the desk as he planted his own broad butt behind it. He tossed some glossy photographs across the green blotter to Longarm, saying, "I hopes you got a good grip on your breakfast. Study 'em anyways, whilst I digs out the vital statistics on the poor son of a bitch."

Longarm's face remained impassive, but his tobacco smoke took on a sort of vomitous taste as he examined the photographs of the Kiowa Kid's mortal remains. By the

13

time the posse had returned with the camera crew the hot sun, coyotes, and carrion crows had joined the ants in worrying the scalped cadaver. Longarm nodded. "Reminds me of the summer of Little Big Horn. Want me to hang on to these, boss? Or was you figuring on framing them for your guest room?"

"They are yourn to keep and cherish, old son," Vail said. "For the dumb bastards went and buried the real thing without so much as a proper medical examination. The coroner of Middle Fork, Dakota Territory, sent me them pretty pictures along with an educated guess that the Sioux arrow in the gent's back kilt him afore he was scalped. According to the yellow sheets on the victim, the jasper posed so delightsome was a drifting gunslick and likely homicidal maniac called the Kiowa Kid."

Longarm said, "That handle's a new one to me, Billy. How come they called him the Kiowa Kid? Was he really a Kiowa, or mayhaps a breed?"

"He's described as just a mean old boy from Texas who left there sudden after raping a Mexican gal and ripping her face off with a busted bottle. Don't have his Christian or surname. By the time the world was aware of his existence he was already acting awful and telling folks to call him the Kiowa Kid. The few living witnesses to his passing say he was a skinny dark white boy in his late teens or early twenties. You can't tell from them pictures, but his hair was curly black, back in the days when he still had some."

Longarm nodded. "I can see he was scalped Cheyenne. Did they slice his fingers Cheyenne-style as well?" he asked.

"No. Coyotes must have exposed the bones of his hands like that. The sheriff of Middle Fork says the medicine stripes on the fatal arrow was red, not Cheyenne blue. What I can't figure out is why it *matters!* Just afore whomsoever kilt him, The Kiowa Kid kilt a mess of folk and raped a

14

mess of women. Kilt some of *them* as well, and, worse yet, he stole *horses!* He was a no-good mad-dog son of a bitch riding a day or more ahead of the posse as found him. They were aiming to gun him on sight. But now Washington wants me to send you up to Standing Rock Reservation to question your old pal, White Bull, about the Kiowa Kid's well-deserved death!"

Longarm blew a thoughtful smoke ring before he replied, "Do tell? What am I to do with any Indian as owns up to the deed? Arrest him or pin a medal on him?"

"The night letter instructions don't say," Vail said. "They just want us to check it out. They asked for you, specific, by name. I don't *like* this, Longarm! I smell something rotten in the wind, and I don't mean the Kiowa Kid!"

Longarm put the photographs away in his tobacco-colored tweed frock coat without comment. Vail scowled at the papers in his stubby hands and added, "Why us? Why you? The Standing Rock Reservation ain't in our jurisdiction. They already has a tolerable U. S. marshal up in Bismarck, less than a hundred miles from either Middle Fork *or* the reservation, and he can't be all that busy."

Longarm shrugged. "Well, I do know White Bull personal, albeit calling him my pal might be putting it a mite strong," he said. "We first met up when I captured him that time during the fuss about Custer."

He took a thoughtful drag on his cheroot and added, "Mayhaps the B.I.A. asked for me because I savvy a little Lakota—or, have it your way, Sioux. I do get along better with Indians in general than some of the idjets Washington has riding herd on 'em, and I did get lucky that time investigating the Ghost Dance Movement, remember?"

Vail snorted. "That was at Pine Ridge. Ain't been no such foolishness at Standing Rock, and the B.I.A. never asked shit from us. I checked. These spooky orders come direct from Washington, and I know the spooky gent as signed 'em."

Vail helped himself to a smoke from the cigar humidor on his desk and took his time lighting it as the banjo clock on the wall ticked on for a spell. "I ain't supposed to allow you children to watch your elders acting dirty," Vail said finally. "But I know you ain't much given to office gossip. So I'm going to tell you a secret. The foxy grandpa as ordered me to order you up to Dakota would sell his own mother if a bastard's mother was worth anything much. He outranks me because he's better at kissing ass and playing political chess. So I can't tell him to go to hell. But I can tell *you* to really watch your step this time, old son."

Longarm chuckled. "I've been wondering who writ the regulations calling for me to wear this sissy suit and tie on the job. But, hell, you could be making a chess game out of simple checkers, Billy. What trouble can I get into, just running up to Standing Rock to ask old White Bull how many of his young men have been counting coup of late, despite all Uncle Sam has done for 'em? We both know he'll say he just can't say, whether he can or he can't. I'll file a report to that effect and hop the first train back. I can see from here it's a fool's errand. But I can't see any obvious pitfalls in my path."

Vail said, "It ain't the pitfalls a man *sees* that he *steps* in! I wants your promise that you'll be careful as a virgin on a Saturday night in Dodge. And I don't want you chasing after any side issues, no matter how pretty they wink at you. You just follow them fool orders to the letter and get right back as soon as White Bull's finished lying to you. Hear?"

Vail cocked his head. "I hear Henry out front," he added. "It's about time. This office opens official in less than ten minutes. Go tell Henry to type you up the usual papers

16

you'll need. I got to compose me my own officious letter protesting the waste of my valuesome manpower just to satisfy the curiosity of a tedious fool!"

Longarm rose and stepped out to jaw with the prissy clerk who played the typewriter in the reception room. Henry tried not to let his distaste show as Longarm smiled down at him. The clerk had a grudging respect for Longarm as a lawman, after typing up so many arrest reports for the big, rawboned deputy. But Henry was a natty dresser and, though Longarm tried to look reasonably civilized, at least in town, Henry did not approve of a costume consisting of a tobacco-colored tweed suit worn over stovepipe army boots and under a cross-draw gun rig, topped by a dark brown pan-caked Stetson with more than one bullet hole in it.

Henry nodded primly and said, "I know. A blank check to travel at government expense anywhere on the North American continent. I don't know why I have to type up orders for you, Longarm. You never follow them, anyway."

Longarm said he'd settle for the papers he'd need to get to and from Dakota Territory and remained on his feet, knowing Henry typed fast. The forms were standardized, so Henry could talk as he typed. "I just met a great admirer of yours, Longarm," he said. "Miss Rubinia, the new wait-ress at the Cup and Saucer on Larimer, tells me you and she are going steady."

Longarm frowned thoughtfully and said, "I disremember going *anything* with any gal named so peculiar, Henry. You say she's slinging hash at the Cup and Saucer? Wait a minute. Is she by any chance a redhead, built sort of *Police Gazette*, with a beauty mark on her cheek?"

Henry nodded. "She was when I had breakfast there on my way to work just now. She's a real looker, you lucky dog. But how come you couldn't recall her name or where she worked? *I* surely would if she was *mine!*"

17

Longarm shrugged. "I got a lot on my mind this morning. Would you do me a favor, Henry?"

Henry shot him a suspicious look as he went on typing.

Longarm said, "Miss Rubinia is expecting me to come calling after work this evening. I was wondering if you'd be a pard and sort of drop by to explain how I had to go back out in the field, and sort of console her."

Henry tore a blank out and started another. "I guess so. When shall I tell her she can expect you back? And what do you mean, *console* her?"

"Hell, Henry, how in thunder would I know when I'll be back? If White Bull's band is off the reservation I may wind up chasing them all over Robin Hood's barn! Meanwhile, old Rubinia's sort of, well, warm-natured, and I'd hate to think of her pining all alone and unconsoled, if you follow my drift."

Henry looked shocked—it was easy for him—as he gasped, "You can't mean that the way it sounds! I must be getting a dirty mind from associating with you! Do I look like the kind of man who'd try to steal a friend's girl while he was out of town?"

It wouldn't have been neighborly to tell Henry what kind of man Longarm thought he looked like, so he replied, "I thanks you for calling me your friend, Henry. I admires you, too, and you wouldn't exactly be stealing her. You'd just be helping with the chores, see?"

Henry said firmly, "I'll tell her why you couldn't meet her after work. Your other suggestion is just too grotesque to consider!"

"Well, suit yourself, Henry." Longarm resisted the impulse to add, "You infernal sissy!" as he waited for the clerk to finish.

Henry tore the last sheet out and handed them all to Longarm, saying something about the northbound Burlington and the connections Longarm would have to make to reach the rail stop at the Standing Rock agency.

Longarm had already figured how to get there and, as usual, Henry's route was the complicated one. But he nodded and put the papers away so he could go gather his Winchester, saddle, and possibles from his furnished digs on the unfashionable side of Cherry Creek. As he opened the door to the hallway, Henry cleared his throat and croaked, "Longarm?"

"Yeah, Henry?"

"About that redhead . . . I mean . . ."

"I know what you mean, and a gent never discusses such details about a lady with another gent. So you'll have to find out for yourself, old son. But I will give you a hint. Miss Rubinia purely admires masterful men. So you just act as masterful as you can manage, hear?"

As he left, he heard Henry muttering to himself. "Masterful? Oh, Lord, what am I getting myself into this time?"

Longarm chuckled as he moved on, mildly surprised to learn that old Henry had ever gotten into anything, any time.

Chapter 3

Longarm got off the train at the McIntosh Agency, since it was the stop nearest the frame shack where White Bull was supposed to be residing, if the old rascal and his band were still on the reservation at all.

For obvious reasons, few trains crossing an Indian reservation ever actually stopped. So Longarm was neither alarmed nor surprised to note that his detraining had attracted the attention of a modest crowd.

Most of them were Indians, of course. The kids grinned at him. Their elders just stared. Longarm could understand how they felt. In their day, the Lakota Nation had been feared and respected from the Great Lakes to the Shining Mountains. Now they were charity wards and semi-prisoners of the Great White Father and, while things had improved a lot since the notorious Indian Ring of the Grant administration had been cleaned up, they likely remembered the Shining Times, when life had been less tedious.

A tall, nice-looking brave was standing a little apart, dressed white, save for the feather stuck in the wampum band of his black Stetson, and since he had a federal badge pinned on his denim shirt, Longarm recognized him as a member of the Indian police.

Nobody had offered to help Longarm with the army saddle and possibles unloaded with him. So he let them be, for now, and moved over to ask his fellow lawman where the Indian agent might be.

The Indian policeman's English was as good as Longarm's as he replied. "He and his lady aren't here right now, Longarm. But they told me to be expecting you. Washington wired you was coming, just before they had to go down to the agency at McLaughlin. I'm called Mahto-Tonka. My orders are to see you about and assist you in any way I can."

Longarm held out his hand and said, "I'm proud to meet you, Big Bear. Did the agent say why he had to leave or when he could be expected back?"

The Indian hesitated, then shook hands and said, "They don't tell us much. I am surprised to see you speak my language, Longarm."

"Well, let's not get carried away, Big Bear. We'll do better jawing in American, since I only have a few words of Lakota. But Mahto-Tonka was easy."

The Indian policeman smiled thinly. "I am not a Sioux. I am a Crow. You probably know we speak the same language, even though in the old days we were enemies."

Longarm nodded without comment. He understood now why Big Bear had been standing apart from the others. He knew the Indian policeman had no more to say about Indian policy than he did, but it sure seemed dumb to rub Lakota noses in it even deeper by appointing a man from an enemy nation as the town law.

Big Bear said, "I will show you to the guest quarters up at the Big House. You will want a mount for that saddle when you are ready to do some riding. My station is over there, beyond the trading post. I have plenty of good ponies in the corral out back. I think you will want a big one, eh?"

"If I have to do any riding at all. If White Bull is within walking distance I likely won't. I'll tell you up front that I seem to have been sent on a fool's errand. You and the agent have doubtless already questioned him about that white boy arrowed Hunkpapa about two days' ride from here, right?"

Big Bear shrugged. "The agent spoke to White Bull and wired what he said to Washington. None of them talk to me at all if they can help it."

"I figured that might be the case. Are you riding herd here all alone, Big Bear?" Longarm asked.

"Yes. A Lakota woman used to keep house for the law officer stationed here. She quit when she learned I was of the sparrow-hawk clan. Let me help you with your gear. I could order someone to carry it for you and they would do it, but I get tired of hearing myself called a sister-fucker."

Longarm agreed and the Lakota made room for them—a lot of room—as they walked over to gather up his saddle and possibles. Longarm carried most of it as the Crow led him over to the agent's quarters. It was easy to tell white folks lived there. None of the other frame houses had a lick of paint on the weathered gray siding.

This was neither the result of economy on Uncle Sam's part nor sloth on the part of the local Indians. Indians just didn't hold with painting wood unless they had a medicine reason for it. Wood looked fine to them just the way it came, while coloring any object changed its medicine, for good or evil, and the whitewash Washington favored was the color of a sun-bleached skull.

As the Crow had promised, the guest wing of the agency quarters was spacious, clean, and comfortable. The door to the private quarters of the agent and his wife was, of course, locked. The Crow said Longarm could get his grub at the trading post and cook it on the range in the corner if he wanted. The brass bedstead had been made up with fresh linens, and there was plenty of coal oil in the lamps and a cord of wood out back.

Longarm put his gear down, said he liked the layout fine, and asked about old White Bull. The Crow said he'd show him the way and that it wasn't far.

It only took them a few minutes to walk to the shack on the outskirts of the settlement. A snarly yellow dog came out to cuss at them. Longarm said, "I'll go on in alone. No offense, pard, but I reckon I'd do as well without a Crow sitting in on the powwow."

Big Bear said he understood and that he'd be at the police station when Longarm next needed his services. Longarm walked toward the house, warning the dog that if he so much as tore his pants he'd ask White Bull's old woman to serve him for supper. So the dog just barked away at a safe distance.

As Longarm approached the front porch, the door opened and an old man as tall as Longarm, wearing braids and a blanket, stepped out to stare at him thoughtfully.

Longarm raised his right palm and said, *"How cola,* Tatanka-Sota."

White Bull answered, *"How cola,* Meneaska-Washtay. My heart soars to see you still live, and that you have not forgotten how to speak like a human being, at least a little."

The old man sat down on the edge of his porch and patted the planks at his side. "We had better sit out here. I have been having a fight with my woman and she throws things. I know why you have come. I told everyone who will listen, but they keep bothering me anyway. Hear me, Meneaska-Washtay; I am not an evil person and I never speak with two tongues, even to my enemies. When we used to fight each other in the last days of the Shining Times, did I ever lie to you?"

23

Longarm sat down beside the old chief, took out two cheroots, and handed him one. "Nope, I took your word when you surrendered to us that time, and you never broke it."

White Bull smiled wistfully. "By Wakan Tonka, that was a good fight, wasn't it? *You* talked straight, too, Meneaska-Washtay. I have not forgotten how you kept those blue sleeves from turning the guns on lodges filled mostly with women and children. I have not fogotten that you gave us your word that none of my young men would be hanged if we surrendered honorably, or that your word was good, even when you had to hit that officer in the nose. That is why I still call you Good-American instead of the name the other Meneaska call you."

A china dish skimmed out the open doorway to miss the old man's head by a whisker before smashing on the hard packed dirt of the yard. White Bull explained, "She is angry because I told her I can do nothing about her sister's daughter. The girl was insulted by a crazy person the other day. But it was off the reservation. The crazy person was a Meneaska, like you, but bad. What can I do about it? They have taken my medicine away. I am not a real chief any more. I am just an old man who has no medicine."

"You still have the respect of your people as well as mine, Tatanka-Sota," Longarm said. "It's against federal law to trifle with an Indian lady. Have you filed a complaint?"

"No. My woman wants me to. That is why she keeps throwing things at me. But I know that if I protest as a chief of the Hunkpapa I will lose even more medicine, when nobody pays attention to my words and my people see how weak I am."

Longarm couldn't dispute that. "I came to find out what you know about that Hunkpapa arrow imbedded in a white

24

boy not too far from here, Chief," he said.

"I know," White Bull said. "Hear me. None of my young men did it. I fear most of them no longer know how to make an arrow fly true. Nobody hunts with arrows any more. Even if they did, that white was not killed by a hunting arrow. Your people described the fletching of the shaft they found in that white up beyond Middle Fork. It was a war arrow. Owl feathers make an arrow fly silently. Red medicine stripes make it strike true. I used to kill Crow and Snakes with arrows like that. But hear me—that was long ago, before the fight with Custer at the Greasy Grass. Before you Meneaska had your war between the blue and gray clans. Killing a man is serious business. If one of my young men rode out to kill anyone today, he would take a *rifle!* You can buy a good Spencer repeater over at the trading post. I told the other people who bothered me all this. It makes me cry blood to hear a man as wise as *you* asking such foolish questions, Meneaska-Washtay!"

Longarm said, "Makes me feel a fool, too. But orders is orders, old son. Let me ask you something about civilized warfare, Lakota style. Ain't it true that when a Lakota gent leaves his personal medicine in a corpse as a calling card, then rides off with the corpse's hair, he's supposed to perform certain rites and brags before he can count coup on the cuss, fair and square?"

A teapot sailed out the door, followed by a high-pitched scream of feminine rage from inside the house. White Bull ignored it.

"That is how I know none of my people could have done it," he replied. "Have you any idea how we *hate* your people, my son?"

"Well, some do seem sort of surly, Chief."

"Hear me. We hate your guts and gizzards! We old men dream of how things might have been if we knew then what we know now. The young men have been raised on tales of glory, when we were real men, not weaklings forced to eat scraps from the table of the people who beat us, *beat us*, oh, how you beat us, and how you still mistreat us!"

"Now, don't get your bowels in an uproar, Chief. I told you when we first met up that we lived in changing times and that I was sorry as hell about old Columbus taking the wrong turn on his way to India. What's done is done, and we're talking about Hunkpapa arrow in the back of a hairless white boy."

White Bull said flatly, "If one of my young men killed him I would know. He would have insisted on showing the scalp to me as he claimed his coup, and, I will tell you truly, I would have *given* it to him, and proclaimed a scalp dance! But nothing like that happened. Damn it."

Longarm nodded. "Needless to say, as you were all enjoying said rites, the Indian police would have arrived, with or without a troop of U. S. Cavalry to arrest all concerned. So ain't it possible some Lakota with a long memory but modest legal training could have done the deed sort of on the sly?"

A rolling pin flew out the door to strike the old man across the shoulder blades. He winced but said nothing about it as he explained to Longarm, "An Indian, killing for vengeance without glory, would never have taken the scalp. You people just don't understand about scalping. What is a scalp that hasn't been consecrated by the proper medicine rites? It's just a hairy patch of poor leather. Go back and tell the Great White Father how dumb he is, Meneaska-Washtay. We know nothing, *nothing*, about that killing on the prairie a good two days' ride from here. I have spoken."

A teacup shattered against the back of the old Indian's skull. He rose majestically and added, "Excuse me. I have to go inside and beat that foolish woman."

Longarm rose, too, but insisted, "One more question, Chief. Would anyone here at Standing Rock know if some other Indians, say Cheyenne, were in these parts?"

White Bull nodded but said, "I heard he was scalped in the manner of Those Who Cut Fingers. There are no Cheyenne around here any more. The nearest Cheyenne were herded down to Rosebud by the blue sleeves two or three summers ago. There are no Indians on the open range this summer. I would have heard if there were, and I do not lie."

Having said all he had to say, the old man marched into the house. Longarm turned away as he heard the dismal sounds of a woman being whipped within an inch of her life.

He ran the whole conversation through his memory a couple of times as he walked back to the agency. The old chief made more sense than Washington did. The law two days or more off at Middle Fork might or might not know a little more. But Billy Vail had told him just to come up here, take the old chief's statement, and head back to Denver. For once, Longarm meant to obey his orders to the letter.

He would have, too, had His Highness, Prince Deltorsky, had the sense to mind his manners while Longarm was anywhere near Dakota Territory.

Chapter 4

Longarm found Big Bear where the Crow had said he'd be. The Indian police station was a one-room nothing-much near the more imposing trading post. It was furnished with one chair, one desk, and a big patent put-together cell-cage that filled up most of the shack, but happened to be empty at the moment. Big Bear got up from behind the desk, politely, to offer his white guest the one chair. He said, "You don't have to tell me what White Bull said. Would you like to pick your pony now?"

Longarm shook his head. "Don't even want that bentwood chair, pard. Don't mean to stay that long. Told you it was a fool's errand. But I done it, and now it's time to catch me a southbound train. Do you have a railroad timetable in that desk?"

"No, but I can tell you when the next train from the north crosses the reservation, within an hour either way. Ought to be one passing through between four and five this afternoon."

Longarm nodded.

Then Big Bear added, "Of course, they never *stop* on the reservation."

Longarm frowned. "Sure they do. I just got off one, didn't I?"

Big Bear grimaced. "That's because you asked them to. Of course they'll stop a train for a *white* man. But when passing through a settlement inhabited by Indians, they tend to speed up if anything."

Longarm smiled incredulously and asked, "How in thunder is anyone supposed to ever *leave* this reservation, then?"

"They're not, without permission. When and if the agent here wants a train to stop, he wires the request up or down the line to the railroad dispatchers. He has a regular telegraph outfit over to his quarters."

"That's more like it. I know how to tap out Morse. Do you have a key to the locked-up part of the big house, Big Bear?"

"No. I told you nobody could go in there while the boss is away."

"Damn it, old son, you're talking to the U. S. law."

Big Bear shrugged. "What law do you think *I'm* working for, Mexico? I told you I don't have a key. If you try to break in I'll have to try and arrest you, and one of us could get hurt."

Longarm smiled thinly. "Let's not get proddy, pard. I never said nothing about breaking and entering on your beat. How far would I have to ride if I took you up on that pony and headed someplace where the fool train stops regular?"

The Crow let out the breath he'd been sort of holding in, thoughtfully, and said, "The nearest place you might be able to flag down a train would be Lemmon—about eighty miles, following the tracks. You could save some time on the prairie by cutting cross-country to Shields, on Cedar Creek, and catching the other branch. That would be, let's see, about fifty miles."

Longarm swore softly and said, "There has to be a better way. What if I was to just stand over there by the loading platform and wave me a red flag at the locomotive as she come down the tracks this afternoon?"

The Crow shrugged. "You could try. But I doubt they'd stop. Sioux kids are always waving or throwing things at the trains as they cross the reservation, Longarm. No offense, but you're sort of sunburnt and rangy, for a white man. So they'd be likely to take you for a drunken Sioux and, like I said—"

"Oh, hell," Longarm cut in, "I'd best give the agent at least overnight to get back and do it the easy way. Them quarters you just showed me beats camping on the open plain, as well as figuring out how to return your horse. You reckon they'll be back that soon?"

"They didn't say. But they must plan on coming back some day. They might know at the trading post. The trader folk are white, so the agent's woman *talks* to *them*."

Longarm said he needed some rations if he meant to stay overnight, anyway. As he started to leave, he looked thoughtfully at the Crow and added, "This ain't my business, Big Bear, and I can see how a gent in your position might feel put-upon. But I've learned you can catch more flies with honey than you can with vinegar, and I notice you keep calling the folks around here Sioux. Didn't nobody ever tell you the Lakota don't fancy that title much?"

The Crow grimaced and said, "I know Sioux is an insulting term in Chippewa. You should hear some of the things the bastards call *me!* Besides, this *is* the Standing Rock Sioux Reservation, on paper. They'll just have to get used to being Sioux. It's what everybody else calls them— and they sure deserve the name."

Longarm shrugged. "Well, suit yourself. But if I made a habit of calling folks something as means something between enemy and snake in the grass, I wouldn't be all that surprised when they failed to invite me to supper."

He left the Crow lawman to ponder his words as he pondered them some himself on the way next door to the trading post. He knew the government called the Lakota

Sioux, officially. It was just another example of the Indian policy made up by folks back East who'd never seen an Indian. In fairness to the B.I.A., such misconceptions had likely been natural enough in the old days, moving west. Neither the Lakota nor Nadene Nations had been given to long conversations with strangers on what they'd regarded as their own hunting grounds. So many a scout with an arrow through his hat had settled for asking friendlier Indians he *could* talk to what one called those sullen sons of bitches up ahead, and, since said friendlier Indians had considered them sons of bitches, too, the Lakota had been named Sioux by the Chippewa and the Nadene had been dubbed Apache by the Pueblo.

Longarm went into the trading post. It was set up like most general stores, albeit stocked with more trashy cheap stuff than one would have found in the poorest white settlement. He knew that, like the other clashes in culture, it was hard to fix the blame on either side. The Indian traders were licensed by the B.I.A. and weren't supposed to take advantage of the Indians. On the other hand, the traders, like any other businessmen, were entitled to make money. So they stocked what they figured they could best make a quick profit on. Indians did favor bright colors, didn't have the same eye for value as white settlers might have, and didn't have much money to spend to begin with. The results were piles of shoddy blankets that would turn from Turkish red to pink the first time they were washed, bright ribbon bows that tended to fall apart as well as fade in the sun, jeans made cheap, with running stitches that split the seams if a man tried to do a day's real work in them, and so forth. Items for sale that couldn't be produced cheap without hurting anyone, like flour, salt, canned beans, and such, were priced higher than any white would have stood for in a gold mining camp.

Longarm worked his way through piles to the counter at

31

the back of the cavernous interior, determined not to say anything nasty no matter how disgusted he felt.

His chore turned out to be easier than he expected when a nice-looking little white gal with straw-blonde hair, big blue eyes, and a winning smile asked, "May I help you, sir? Oh, you're a white man!"

Longarm smiled back. "Your stock just rose in my book, ma'am. For I see you have good manners despite what you sell to these poor Lakota."

"Don't you mean Dakota? My uncle says I'm not to call them Sioux because Dakota is their real name."

"Well, mayhaps your uncle ain't such a bad cuss, neither, though his accent's wrong for this far west. The tribes further east said Dakota. The Hunkpapa Tetons call themselves Lakota. It means friends. That's why your uncle's right about not callin 'em Sioux. Ah, is that uncle about, ma'am? I'm Deputy U. S. Marshal Custis Long and this visit is partly official."

The blonde shook her head and said, "He and the Krugers went down to the McLaughlin agency on business, sir. I'm Polly Bean. I'm just out here for the summer. I've only been helping out, here at the trading post. I fear I don't really know much about Indians *or* shopkeeping."

He started to ask who the Krugers were, then he remembered that was the name of the local agent and his woman. "Call me Custis," he said. "I ain't old enough to be a sir, yet. I wanted to talk to somebody here who'd likely know more than you do about tribal matters. But I can see this just ain't my day, Miss Polly. So I'll settle for some provisions and smokes. I'm staying out in the guest quarters at least for tonight, so I'll need—let's see—coffee, biscuits, beans, and mayhaps a can of tomato for dessert. I smokes any cheroots as don't run more than three for a nickel."

She said she'd be proud to serve him. But just then a fat

old Lakota woman came in, pushing past him to belly up to the counter.

Polly said, "Oh, dear."

"Me want ten pounds flour," the Indian woman said.

"Mrs. Blue Feather, you know what my uncle told you about your line of credit," the white girl said.

The Lakota woman insisted, "Trader not here. Me want flour. Me want flour *now!*"

"Mrs. Blue Feather, you know I can't extend credit to anyone on my own, and your unpaid bill is awfully high," Polly said.

The fat Indian woman wailed, "My children hungry. My children no savvy money. You give me just five pounds flour and I pay you sure on allotment day, yes?"

The white girl sighed. "Oh, dear," she said again as the older woman began to cry. Longarm reached into his pocket, but before he could make the gesture, Polly went on. "For heaven's sake don't cry, Mrs. Blue Feather. Look, if I give you some flour, you have to promise me you'll not tell anyone. Not even my uncle when he comes back. All right?"

"All right. All good. You good person, Funny Hair."

The blonde muttered, "I think *fool* is the word we're groping for," as she reached under the counter and produced a ten-pound sack of flour. She slid it across to Mrs. Blue Feather, who simply picked it up with a triumphant smile and turned to leave without another word.

Polly looked up wearily at Longarm. "They never even say thank you. I suppose you think that was mighty foolish of me, right?"

Longarm smiled. "She said what you was, ma'am. I couldn't put it any better. But hold on—do you folks keep a *list* of Lakota owing money here?"

She said, "Of course. The Lakota aren't the best money managers in the world. So they always spend their cash allotment from the B.I.A. long before the next one is due. We have to extend every household a line of credit to get them through to the next allotment day. Most pay up when they get their monthly allotment, then more or less piddle the rest away. That woman who just suckered me hasn't paid her tab in six months, though. I know I was foolish, but what can one do, let children go hungry just because their mother is a poor manager?"

"We've all agreed you're a good person, Miss Polly. Could I have me a look at the current line of credit as well as the one from—let's see—two months back?"

She looked puzzled but nodded, opened a drawer, and rummaged out a pair of nickel notepads, asking him what he expected to find.

"Missing names," he said. "You just go ahead and fill my order and I'll pay today, Miss Polly."

She proceeded to pile things on the counter as Longarm scanned the lines of credit. She finished first. There were a lot of names to read off. When he'd finished, he handed the two listings back and said with a frown, "Well, it *sounded* like a good notion."

"What were you looking for?" she asked.

He said, "I've reason to suspicion one or more Lakota jumped this reservation, recent. But save for that Crow policeman who come *on* the reservation earlier this month, the two listings are identical. Everyone who was buying on credit a couple of months ago is still running up a tab this month."

She nodded. "Oh, I see. That means nobody from Standing Rock has gone wild again, right?"

"Not exactly. It means anyone who has is acting sneaky about it. I was asked to look into a Hunkpapa arrow winding up where it shouldn't have, about two days' ride from here. A sneak could ride that far and back without missing the family shopping day. I notice most of 'em buy in bulk, hardly more than one day a week."

"That's true. But wait. If you know the exact day someone was two days' ride away, and someone *else* was in here stocking up on salt and flour..."

"You're right. Process of elimination would only tell us who it *couldn't* have been. That'd still leave plenty as it *could* have, and these accounts are sort of tedious reading material. Could I borrow them to go over again later on, as I sip me some coffee and such?"

She handed them back with a smile and he put them away with a nod of thanks. Then he stared down wistfully at the provisions she'd gathered for him and asked, "Don't you have Arbuckle coffee, ma'am? I tried this brand once, and, no offense, it may say coffee on the can, but it sure tasted more like tanbark."

She sighed and said, "I'm afraid our usual customers can't afford good coffee, Custis. My uncle says they put flour in it, anyway."

"Well, they have unusual views on how coffee is supposed to taste. Have you ever smoked their shongasha?"

"No, but I know it's what they call tobacco," she replied.

"They got unusual views on what a smoke ought to taste like, too. I see these cheap cheroots are regular trade tobacco, though, so I'm ahead of the game on that. Never heard of this brand of tomato, but the picture on the label can't mean it's full of spinach. How come you gave me dried beans in a sack, ma'am?"

"You said you wanted beans, didn't you?"

"I did, but...Never mind; I was a fool to think a trading post sold canned beans when you can buy 'em in bulk so cheap. Where's the biscuits?"

"I fear we don't have any pastry products already baked, Custis. You see, they prefer to make their own sort of odd bread, and—"

He cut her off with a sigh of understanding and said,

35

"I'll settle for a pound of wasna, then."

"Wasna?"

"Pemmican. I know a packing house in Chicago makes up pemmican sausage to sell to prospectors, Indians, and such, and they ought to be ashamed of themselves, but at least it sticks to the ribs."

She nodded. "Oh, we do have some pemmican. I've never tried it."

As she placed what looked like a long, dark turd on the counter between them Longarm said, "Don't. Like I said, it beats going hungry, but that's about all one can say for trade pemmican. The wasna the Indians used to make themselves, with real buffalo and wild berries, tasted like something else entire."

He gathered up his dismal purchases, paid way the hell too much for them, and left for his temporary quarters. When he got there he found someone waiting for him, seated on the steps and dressed in the old-fashioned white deerskins and beadwork of an unmarried Lakota gal. He nodded pleasantly and his visitor rose politely to announce in a soft contralto voice, "I am called Pretty Blankets. White Bull is the husband of my aunt. She tells me you are a good person with strong medicine. I have been insulted and mistreated by a man of your people. Nobody here will do anything about it, and I have been weeping blood in vain!"

Longarm nodded. "Come on in and tell me about it while I put these things down, Miss Pretty Blankets. Have you tried filing your complaint with your own law, Big Bear?"

Pretty Blankets waited until they were inside before going on. "You can't be serious. Big Bear is a *Crow!* How could a Lakota girl ask a dirty Crow to defend her honor? Haven't you heard Crow don't punish people for incest? They used to be Lakota, themselves, until our people drove them from the nation because one of their chiefs slept with his own sister."

Longarm put the supplied on the bed table and waved Pretty Blankets to a seat on the made-up bedstead. "That was a long spell back, if it ever happened, Miss Pretty Blankets, and the Crow tell a different tale. I won't go into what they say about *your* tribal customs, since Big Bear likely has enough on his plate as it is. I don't know if I can do anything for you or not, until I hear what happened."

Pretty Blankets smoothed the blankets of the bed sensuously with a well-kept but sort of rawboned brown hand. "My, this bed feels so nice under a girl's behind, and the springs don't make any noise at all, do they?"

He said, "Can't say. Ain't tried to make 'em talk to me yet," as he regarded his fancy-dressed visitor with more interest and some dismay. Pretty Blankets was dressed mighty pretty, and neither the face nor what he could make out of the figure under the loose-fitting deerskins was exactly ugly. But somehow Longarm had never fancied tall, skinny gals with sort of hatchet faces, and Pretty Blankets' long beaked nose offered an awesome barrier to serious kissing. "Let's talk about the white man who mistreated you, ma'am," he said, as he tried to ignore the batting lashes and bedroom eyes of his guest.

"It happened the other day when I was riding my little pony out to the northwest to gather herbs," Pretty Blankets said.

"Were you off the reservation?"

"Well, maybe a *little* off the reservation. There's no boundary fence and we're not exactly prisoners, you know."

"Right. You were riding along, minding your own herb business—and then what happened?"

"I came upon a Meneaska cowboy. At least, I think he was a cowboy. He was wearing funny clothes. He was off his mount, looking at its off front hoof. I think his mount had thrown a shoe. I rode over and offered to help. But he spoke neither your language nor mine."

Longarm nodded and said, "Sounds like a Red River breed. We ain't all that far from the Canada line. What happened then?"

"He made advances to me. I was only trying to be friendly. But he took me in his arms, said something in that strange tongue, and began to—well—grope at me."

Longarm nodded soberly. From the smoke signals Pretty Blankets was sending with those smouldering dark eyes he could well see how a lonely rider on the prairie might have tried to cut through a language barrier with uncouth gestures. He was trying to think how he could put it most delicately when Pretty Blankets added, "Then his face got red, like a crazy person's. He shook me, punched me to the ground, and kicked me as I lay there, stunned and sobbing. It was awful. I was so frightened!"

Longarm frowned. "I'd say you had every right to be, ma'am. What happened then? Did he . . . well, I can't come up with a politer word than rape."

Pretty Blankets said, "No. He kicked me and kicked me. Then he spit on me and rode off laughing. I have told everyone he must be a crazy person and that the other girls are in danger. But nobody will do anything. Would you arrest him for me, Meneaska-Washtay? I would do anything, anything at all, if you would avenge my honor!"

As if to make the offer more obvious, Pretty Blankets lay back and managed to expose one long brown thigh. Longarm ignored the twinge of interest in his groin to say firmly, "Fooling with Indian gals is a federal offense, no offense, so let's keep this conversation proper, Miss Pretty Blankets. Sit up decent and tell me more about the cuss who insulted your femininity by spitting on it. What did he look like, exactly?"

Pretty Blankets shrugged. "Oh, you know—a man of your people, though not as pretty. He wasn't a Metis from

38

Canada. He wore a big fur hat. He wore a long gray coat, like the blue sleeves wear in the winter, even though it was a warm summer day. The coat had funny things on the chest." Pretty Blankets giggled and went on, "If a girl wore a coat like that they would tickle her tits. It looked like he wore cartridge loops on his chest, over his nipples, but that is a silly place to carry bullets, don't you agree?"

Longarm pursed his lips as he tried to picture something that fit Pretty Blanket's odd description. Finally he said, "Well, that don't sound like any outfit *I* ever rid with. I've seen pictures of Russian cavalry troops that dress so odd, but that can't be what he was. I know there used to be some Russians out in the Pacific Northwest. But I'd hardly expect to find one in Dakota messing with Lakota gals. You may be right about him being a lunatic. He sounds like an escapee from a traveling circus."

He thought some more and added, "I'll tell you what, Miss Pretty Blankets. I'll put your complaint and his description out on the wire. Anybody dressed so funny and acting so wild won't get far before someone ropes and ties him."

"You won't go after him yourself?"

"Can't, Miss Pretty Blankets. I've done what I come here to do and my office is expecting me back. But I ain't ignoring your complaint. I said I'd put her on the wire, and when they catch him the B.I.A. will see he's punished. Attacking wards of the U. S. government is a serious offense."

Pretty Blankets rose, moved over to lean dangerously near, and said huskily, "What if a girl offers herself willing, Meneaska-Washtay?"

He showed Pretty Blankets out firmly and bolted the door before taking off his coat and tossing it over the bed rail. "Now, just you simmer down, old organ grinder. In the

39

first place she wasn't all that good-looking. In the second, you and me didn't come up here to molest wards of the government!" he told himself.

His dawning erection paid no more attention to him than he meant to pay to it as he sat on the bed, which was still warm from Pretty Blankets' sassy tail, and consulted his watch. It was going on five-thirty and, sure enough, he heard the distant wail of a locomotive whistle. The southbound was running late but running fast as it crossed the reservation.

He got back to his feet and went to the window to watch, wistfully, as the train he should have been on by now whipped through McIntosh Agency. He muttered, "Shit. There ain't a saloon or even a library in this settlement, and the sun ain't even close to setting."

It was too early to consider eating, even if he had had anything decent to eat. He killed some time by starting the wood-burning range and putting a coffeepot he found in a cupboard on to heat up. Then he made sure the door to the outside was bolted secure, moved to the one leading into the main house, and took out his pocketknife to see what he could about that, muttering, "I know, I know, this is likely illegal, and mayhaps even impolite. But there's a telegraph set somewhere on the other side and I don't want to come all the way back if the office wants me to follow up on some of these unexpected loose ends."

It was just as well Longarm toted a badge as well as a knife with a blade that could have gotten a lesser mortal arrested. It only took him a few moments to pick the lock and let himself into the agent's quarters. He found himself in the kitchen, but he resisted the temptation to look for decent rations. He knew they'd be there, but burglary was not what he had in mind.

He moved from room to room, saw the sheets in the

bedroom were rumpled as if the agent and his wife had left without bothering to neaten up for unexpected company, and finally found what he was looking for. The Indian agent's office came with a telegraph set mounted on one end of his big work desk.

Longarm sat down, picked up the earphones, and had a listen. There was nothing on the line. He moved to switch it on and saw that the set was already turned on. But the line couldn't be dead. He'd already noted that a wire ran over here from the poles along the tracks. If the trains were running, the wires were working. Trains didn't pass through a telegraph block when the lines were dead.

He stood up for a better look at the wet cells on the shelf above the desk. Then he swore. The wet cells were empty as well as dusty. The damn fool agent had either let them go dry or, more likely, emptied them before leaving. The acid went on eating at the plates whether one used the set or not, and new parts took time getting out here.

He knew battery acid was shipped and stored as dry powder packed in little brown bottles. So he searched for some in the office. When he found none, he went back to take the pot off the range before he buckled down to searching the whole damned house from top to bottom.

By the time he'd satisfied himself there wasn't a single jar of fresh battery acid on the premises it was dark outside and he had a lower opinion of the housekeeping of the agent's woman.

The attic was filled with dusty junk and cobwebs. Ashes and papers were strewn about messy, downstairs, and something had spoiled in the dirt-floored cellar below. There were all sorts of jars stored on pine shelves down there. Some had fallen to the floor and busted open to go bad. None of them had any battery acid in them.

He gave up and went back to start the coffee making

over. When he got the water boiling and opened the can from the trading post he knew he'd been right about that brand smelling more like tanbark than anything else. He tossed a fistful in anyway and hoped for the best. He wasn't hungry enough yet to try the trade pemmican. By the time the dried beans would cook from scratch he meant to be long gone.

He lit the coal-oil lamp and sat down on the bed with a fresh smoke to go through the charge accounts from the trading post again at his leisure. There figured to be a lot of that going around here before he'd be able to leave.

The debts had been recorded in two hands, mostly feminine. It looked like Miss Polly's uncle was taking advantage of her visit to let her mind the counter most of the time. He took out his own notebook and made notes of Indians who'd bought on time too close to the time in question to be suspects. When he'd finished, he'd learned the trade coffee tasted as bad as it smelled and he still had over a hundred-odd Lakota who could have been most anywhere when the Kiowa Kid took that arrow in his back.

He tossed the tedious task aside and told himself to forget it. He knew without being able to ask that Billy Vail wouldn't want him to waste time on a long, drawn-out investigation when, even if they found out who'd killed the wanted outlaw, they probably couldn't do much to him. The only real mystery after all this time was why the gent who'd put the Kiowa Kid on the ground hadn't stepped forward to claim full credit.

By now everyone in these parts knew about the killing, and knew the dead man had been killed one jump ahead of a posse packing a murder warrant on him. White Bull had been right about it being a deed most Indians would want to brag on. So what in thunder could it all add up to?

"Killer was wanted, too, for something else," Longarm

told his tin cup as he put it aside, still half filled with awful brew. He lit a smoke to get rid of the taste as he tried that notion a couple of ways for the right fit. It fit more than one way, some of them interesting. He had to know a mite more before he could even make an educated guess which fit best, or whether Billy Vail wanted him to follow up on any of them. He was getting hungry now, but still not hungry enough to chew trade pemmican. If he took Big Bear up on that loan of a pony, he could make her to Middle Fork and, better yet, a telegraph office, before he starved to death.

He started cleaning up and putting things back the way he'd found them. A full moon had already risen and figured to stay up there most of the night. If he borrowed *two* mounts, and switched back and forth as he rose, a normal two days' ride in one night wasn't impossible. And anything beat just sitting here like a bump on a stump until that infernal agent and his woman got back to show him where in hell they'd hidden the battery acid.

But his planned departure was delayed by a knock on the door. Longarm opened it to see Miss Polly standing there with a smile on her face and a tray of fresh-cooked grub in her hands.

Chapter 5

Polly said, "It's supposed to be a family secret, but my uncle does stock real coffee for personal consumption, and I baked more biscuits and cake this morning than I can possibly eat all by myself. I hope you won't tell on me for slicing into a fresh ham?"

Longarm took the tray from her and put it on the bed. "I hardly ever tell on angels of mercy, Miss Polly," he said.

He didn't comment on the fact that he could smell that the biscuits and upside-down cake were fresh from the oven. The neighborly little gal had doubtless started mixing the dough the minute he'd stepped out her door. But a lady who didn't want to seem forward was entitled to her white fibs.

He remained standing, politely, expecting her to leave, but Polly sat down on her end of the bed and commenced pouring coffee into the two cups she'd brought along. So he sat down across the tray from her and dug right in. Like most men raised country, Longarm wasn't given to table conversation until after dessert. But she must have already eaten some, for she chattered away at him as he devoured the first decent grub he'd had all day. He had to answer, just to be polite, when she asked if it was true that a body could get a year in prison for deserting a tribe of Indians.

44

He washed down a mouthful of ham and biscuit with decent coffee and replied, "That's *sheep* you're talking about, ma'am. Colorado and most other states out here will give you a year and a day at hard for running off to leave a herd of sheep untended on the range. The laws were passed to discourage a prevalent practice. Lots of old boys sign on for a summer of sheep-herding without knowing what they're getting into. I don't think the laws apply to leaving *Indians* untended on the range. Why do you ask?"

She looked away. "My uncle said someone had to stay here and be responsible until he or the agent got back," she told him. "I know I promised, but I was pressured into it at the time, and since then I've had time to reconsider."

"Reconsider what? Were you planning on lighting out, Miss Polly?"

She nodded. "I knew almost as soon as I came out here that I'd made a mistake. My uncle and I had a heated discussion just before he and the others left. I told him I meant to go back East. But he begged me to stay until he came back from McLaughlin and, like a fool, I agreed."

Longarm nodded sagely. "I know the feeling. I've been fool enough to make promises in my time, too."

"Do you always keep them, Custis?" Polly asked.

"Yep. Have to. If a man don't stand by his own word, whose word can he hold good?"

She looked like she was fixing to blubber up on him, so he added gently, "Of course, a *gal's* word ain't as binding, since it's understood that she-males are changeable by nature. Who was you aiming to leave in charge of the trading post when you left, Miss Polly? And, more important, how were you fixing to leave? Trains don't stop here much, and the nearest place they do is a mighty smart ride from here."

He saw that made her thoughtful, so he added, "Your uncle and the agent can't stay forever down to McLaughlin,

45

whatever they're doing down there. When the agent comes back he can wire the train to stop, and by the way, do you stock any battery acid over to the trading post?"

"Battery acid? I don't think so. What on earth would Indians want with battery acid?"

"Never mind. Dumb question. Reckon the agent just run out and he may be bringing some back from the agency to the south. My point, Miss Polly, is that you'd do better waiting till the other white folks get back."

She shook her head stubbornly. "I don't ever want to see my uncle again. I gave into his pleas at the moment, knowing we were both upset and mayhaps not thinking too clearly. But now that I've calmed down and thought it over more than once, I just don't ever want to have anything to do with him again."

Longarm tried the cake, found it was delicious, and swallowed before he said, "I did notice, going through the books, that he had you doing more work behind the counter than a gal on vacation might have expected. By the way, I noticed something odd in the records you let me go over. A Lakota called Falling Sky charged a peck of salt on the day the posse figured the Kiowa Kid met up with a surly brave. So Falling Sky couldn't have been the one. But in my line of work we look for odd changes in personal habits and I notice that while last month old Falling Sky was running up an awesome tab, this month he's barely bought enough on time to matter. You reckon he's on a diet or something?"

Polly laughed. "I think I can explain that. His eldest daughter, Dancing Antelope, seems to have reformed."

He shot her a quizzical look.

"He has three teenage daughters," she explained. "The eldest has, or had, taking ways. It's not polite to accuse a regular customer of shoplifting. So every time Dancing Antelope sneaked something from the trading post, we just put it on her father's tab. I think my uncle must have spoken to her father about it. I haven't seen her in the post for some time now."

Longarm shrugged and said, "Well, so much for that mystery. I know it's none of my business, but I can't help being a mite curious about this family dispute you've been having with your uncle."

She hesitated, then blushed. "I didn't think I'd ever be able to tell anyone, but you're so understanding and, well, I *have* to tell *someone*."

She stopped, as if gathering her thoughts. Longarm said not a word.

She nodded as if he'd urged her to go on and said, "Uncle Dave *is* my *uncle*, even though I hadn't seen him since I was a child. When my Dad wrote that I was thinking of coming out here this summer to see the West for myself, Uncle Dave said he'd be happy to put me up and look out for me. So I jumped at the chance."

"Then you discovered your vacation figured to be spent working hard, for free, in a dusty Indian agency, with no young white folks your own age to talk to. Right?"

"Oh, that part wasn't bad. I have found it interesting to meet wild Indians and I don't mind working for my keep, but...But, damn it, Uncle Dave *is my uncle!*"

Longarm nodded soberly. "Well, a man has needs, and since President Hayes reformed the B.I.A., he'd have to watch his step with the Indian gals, Miss Polly."

Her face flushed a deeper red. "It would still be incest, even if he wasn't a dirty old man who only shaves once a week!"

Longarm sipped some coffee, letting her get it off her chest her own way in her own good time. Said chest was heaving under her thin calico dress in a way that made him feel a certain sympathy for her dirty old uncle. As a lawman,

47

Longarm got to snoop about more than most, so he knew only too well how common her problem was in many a lonesome sod house or isolated mining camp.

She lowered her eyes and said, "I guess, in a way, it was partly my own fault. That's why I feel ashamed to ever face Uncle Dave again."

"How come, Miss Polly? You wasn't the one as made the suggestion, was you?"

"Good God, no! He tried to get in bed with me! But, you see, when I first came out, he was so understanding and friendly that I did something foolish. With nobody else to talk to, I confided certain things about my past that I never would have told my parents. You see, I came out here mostly to get over a broken engagement. The boy I was engaged to and I were engaged indeed. I might have known that once a girl lets any man know she's not pure, he's bound to entertain certain ideas. But, good heavens, he was *kin!*"

Longarm put the last of the cake away and washed it down with the last coffee before he said gently, "I understand your feeling, Miss Polly. I suspicion I understand your poor old uncle's feelings as well. He's likely as embarrassed by his unnatural mistake as you are. Nothing makes a man feel more foolish than exposing his feelings to a gal as says no, firm. Right now he's likely feeling as red-faced about facing you again as you are about him. But since the matter's been settled and you've both had time to simmer down, it's my guess than when he comes back you'll find he won't ever mention it again."

He lit an after-supper smoke without asking her permission, since it was his quarters. "You'd best stay at least until he can take the key to the trading post from you, awkward or not," he added. "If you were to leave it untended, he'd doubtless return to find it an empty shell. The

48

only law here, with the agent gone, is a poor Crow with little or no control over folks as don't talk to him."

She still looked stubborn. So he asked, "Are you really *that* mad at him?"

She sniffed. "You don't understand. It's not just Uncle Dave's feelings I have to worry about. I have feelings of my *own!* It was easy enough to be pure before I started—well, all right, sleeping regularly with a man back home. But—oh, this is awful, but I have to tell somebody! I'm not sure I'll be able to say no if he climbs in bed with me again."

Longarm smiled crookedly and moved the tray over to the end table. "Welcome to the human race, Miss Polly. Ain't it hard to go without it for a spell, once you've learned to like it?"

She covered her face with her hands and bawled, "I never should have told you! You men are all alike!"

He nodded. "Yep, we're as bad as women. But don't worry. I hardly ever leap at pretty gals uninvited, and I said I understood your mixed-up feelings."

She lowered her hands and stared at him teary-eyed as she asked him, "Do you? I doubt that very much."

He snubbed out his smoke, reached out to trim the lamp, and, as he plunged the room into darkness, reached out for her as well. Polly gasped and stiffened in his arms, so he didn't struggle with her. "I don't aim to do anything you don't want me to, Miss Polly," he said. "Do you want me to stop?"

She sobbed, threw her arms around him, and they were too busy for a spell to talk about what she might or might not want. But Longarm got the distinct impression that the poor love-starved little gal needed it bad.

It wasn't until after he'd undressed them both and given it to her twice that Polly sighed sensuously in his arms and murmured, "I can see why you're so good at tracking down the wayward. You obviously can read minds."

He nibbled her ear, letting his shaft soak in her throbbing privates as he replied, "There's not much of a trick to it, honey. Great minds tend to run in the same channels."

She giggled. "You're a horrid man, thank God. I suppose you think I'm horrid, too?"

"Don't talk dirty, little darling. You ain't done nothing *I* ain't done."

She moved her naked pelvis experimentally. "That's for certain. I'll bet you've seduced a lot of poor girls in your time, you brute."

He started moving in time with her bumps and grinds as he replied. "There you go, talking dirty again. I have learned from sad experience that women tend to do their own seducing, and that I'm just a weak-natured cuss who wouldn't want a pretty gal to take him for a sissy. Are you still trying to tell me you've only done this with one man before me, Polly? Don't forget I'm in a position to know."

She laughed wildly. "Oh, just *do* it, you fool! You know damned well I love it! I came out here to break the habit. But I see there's no use trying and . . . my God, I think I'm coming again! How do you *do* that, Custis?"

"Just practice, I reckon," he answered, as the little blonde went crazy under him for a spell. He started going crazy, too. For, despite being so petite, Polly had a nicely rounded little rump that made for no need to shove a pillow under it to present her all at a welcoming angle. She locked her smooth, shapely little legs around him and they felt comfortable and just right, too, as he pounded to glory while she shuddered in protracted orgasm. He knew it was partly the long train ride up from Denver, but he really couldn't recall a gal in recent memory who fit his body so nicely with her own. Everything about her was just as soft and sweet as the upside-down cake she'd baked as an excuse to get upside-down with him.

When they came up for air, Longarm was planning on how best to suggest some of the wilder positions to a gal who at least pretended to have delicate notions. But Polly spoiled his plans by saying, "I have to get dressed and go back to the trading post."

"I'll go with you. Though this bed suits me fine."

"Heavens, no, you can't!" she said. "What if my uncle returned in the morning?"

"He'll likely be vexed as hell, but we can tell him we're engaged."

"Stop it. You know what I mean. I have to think of my reputation, and he does write regularly to my father. Let me up, Custis. Thanks to you, I know I'll be able to resist temptation with anyone less handsome and well-endowed. My God, I thought *Ralph* was virile, but now that I've had that monstrous thing of yours in me . . ."

He let her out from under him, grimacing in distaste in the darkness. He didn't know why women liked to talk about past misdeeds with other men so much, but they did, and neither he nor any other man he knew really wanted to hear the grim details.

As he lounged naked on the bedspread, Polly dressed with a speed that hinted at past practice. Some gals were like that, too. Women complained about men turning over and falling asleep after lovemaking, but some gals could be just as rude, leaping out of bed to cover their tracks as soon as they'd had their wicked way with a poor abused cuss.

She pecked him on the cheek, sort of sisterly, considering, and lit out for home with the tray and the trading post stuff he'd returned to her. He considered getting up to lock the door after her. He lit the same smoke again instead, muttering, "Waste not, want not. Jesus Christ, I've heard

51

of fast work, but that was something else!"

He was still wide awake, as well as suffering from an only partly sated erection. But it was getting late to consider that moonlight ride now. The moon had moved to a new angle in the sky and was shining her cool rays through one window, lighting things up inside a mite. But, cool as the moonlight looked, he still felt hot. He'd been looking forward to a whole night of Polly's skilled loving. And, damn it, it wasn't even ten o'clock yet!

He'd finished the cheroot and was debating whether to light another one when there came a shy tap on the door. He grinned and got up, thinking, "Like I said, great minds run in the same channels!"

But when he opened the door stark naked it wasn't Polly back for a second helping. Two little Lakota gals were standing there in the moonlight. Both of them were dressed in calico Mother Hubbards and he was dressed in nothing but moonlight. But the damage had been done. They were likely more used to naked flesh than white gals, judging from the way neither screamed. So he asked them to come in and tell him what they wanted.

One spoke English. She said the one who didn't was her sister, and that they were the daughters of Falling Sky. The one doing all the talking said to call her Walking Willow and that her sister was Cherry Basket. The one who didn't speak English shoved past him, jumped on the bed, and hitched her skirts up to cross her bare legs on the rumpled spread. They weren't bad.

Longarm sat down on the bed, too, to sort of hide his semi-erection, so Walking Willow got on the other side of him. It was right cozy. He said he was sorry he only had cheroots and trade coffee to offer. The one who spoke English said, "Thank you, we have eaten. That awful Kongra says you are a lawman with a good heart and big medicine. Is this true?"

He frowned. "Kongra? Oh, right, Crow. I thank Big Bear for the commendation. What can I do for you gals?"

"It is about our sister, Dancing Antelope. She is a bad girl, but we love her, and we think something has happened to her."

He nodded sagely. "Your elder sister is the gal who makes a habit of stealing at the trading post, right?"

Walking Willow clapped her hands with delight and said something in Lakota to her sister, too fast for him to follow. "Oh, you are such a smart person!" she told Longarm. "We are sure you can find out what happened to our naughty sister, now!"

"First you'd better tell me what's happened to her," he said.

"We don't know," the Lakota girl said. "That is why we came to you. That nasty Indian policeman says he can do nothing about a sneak thief who must have jumped the reservation. But we don't think Dancing Antelope would do such a thing. It is true that she steals. She has a spirit who makes her do that. It is true she sometimes leaves the reservation to sell herself and things she has stolen. But she has always come back after having a little fun and getting some money from the Meneaska in Middle Fork or Cedar Creek."

He frowned thoughtfully and said, "She's been fencing stolen goods as far as Middle Fork? Hmm. How long as she been gone this time?"

"Two weeks or more. Our father, Falling Star, thinks she just ran away because he punished her for shaming his name at the trading post. But he has been punishing her for being bad since we were all very small, and she has always come back, once she got over it. We are sure something bad has happened to our bad big sister. Won't you help us?"

"I'm not sure I can, Miss Walking Willow. I'll wire

other law officers to keep an eye out for a Lakota gal wandering about alone on the lone prairie. But from where I sit, I'd say your father's likely right. I'd have heard if anyone had found a young gal out on the range, alive or otherwise, at this late date. I can tell you nobody has. So ain't it more likely she's found a job?"

"Pooh! No whorehouse would hire one of us regular. Those snoops from the B.I.A. cause a fuss when they find Indian girls whoring off the reservation. Besides, Dancing Antelope wouldn't want to be an off-the-blanket Indian. She has too many friends and relations here on Standing Rock. Some bad person must be holding her prisoner, or worse!"

He stared up at the ceiling and muttered, "Why me, Lord?" before he asked Walking Willow if she'd heard about the misadventures of that tall, skinny Pretty Blankets.

Walking Willow sniffed and said, "Oh, her. She's very silly. Men are always pushing her away. Although no Lakota would be rude enough to spit on her. What has that crazy person who abused Pretty Blankets to do with our poor missing sister?"

"I'm not sure," he said, "but we're all agreed the gent she met up with on the prairie acted sort of crazy. Pretty Blankets ain't what I'd call a raving beauty, but considering her kind offer, and how hard up a cowboy can get between paydays, his attitude seems a mite ruder than the situation called for. I managed to defend my virtue from old Pretty Blankets without beating her up."

Walking Willow translated that and both gals laughed like hell. The one doing all the talking giggled at him and asked, "Did Pretty Blankets try to fuck you, Meneaska-Washtay?"

"I got the feeling she had *something* in mind," he said. "But we never. So let's say no more about it. Miss Walking Willow, why is Miss Cherry Basket fooling with my privates?"

Walking Willow giggled again. "I think she wants to fuck you. I would like to, too. But I suppose you think Pretty Blankets is better to look at?"

He leaned back and sighed, "Lord give me strength!" as the one who spoke not a word of English proceeded to translate her own desires by jerking him off teasingly with her skillful little fingers. "Tell her not to do that if she don't want to waste ammunition on the ceiling, damn it!" he said. Walking Willow translated, and Cherry Basket laughed and forked a plump brown naked thigh across him to settle on his shaft with no further discussion in either lingo.

He gasped, "Powder River and let her buck!" as he felt how tight and hot this unexpected but welcome new delight was, once he rose fully to the occasion. Cherry Basket must have been pleasantly surprised, too, for she peeled her Mother Hubbard off over her head, threw her head back, and proceeded to swing her long black hair across his knees like a pony's tail as she posted on his saddle horn, grunting out what sounded like a war chant.

Walking Willow undressed more sedately, saying, "My sister wants me to thank you for her, for having such a nice hard roll of wasna. Will you save some for me when she is finished with it?"

He laughed. "I'll do my best, ma'am, but would you mind shutting up while *I* enjoy it, too?"

Cherry Basket protested in confused Lakota as he rolled her over, with it still in deep, and proceeded to do it right with her on the bottom. He couldn't understand how he'd ever thought, a while back on this same mattress, that he was in the nicest gal parts he'd ever had. For Cherry Basket's strong brown thighs hugged him so tight that nothing could feel righter. But, thanks to his earlier lovemaking, he took longer getting there with the Indian gal, and Cherry Basket took it as a real compliment when she came and he kept going hot and heavy.

Walking Willow got on her hands and knees behind him,

stark, and said, "Oh, your rump is so pretty, going up and down like that in the moonlight!"

She must have meant it, since she began to stroke both buttocks as he moaned and fired his weapon in the moaning little gal under him.

He rolled off, gasping, "I surrender. You gals has counted coup on me for sure, for now."

Walking Willow was all over him, crooning in her own lingo, as she started screwing on top, even better. It was impossible, of course, for any human vagina to feel one bit better than the one he'd just come in, but damned if Walking Willow *wasn't* tighter, or else more muscular inside.

As she moved up and down, sitting tall in the saddle, little Cherry Basket rolled between them, pressed her perky brown breasts against his chest, and started kissing him passionately.

He kissed back, inspiration renewed, and it sure felt wild to be kissing and feeling up one gal while he screwed another—or, rather, while *she* screwed *him*. Longarm just had to lie still amd meet both his makers. Which was just as well. The thin, dry air of the High Plains kept folk from sweating much as they went at whatever, hammer and tongs, but he was glad, this late in the game, that they got to do most of the worrying about breathing. From the way they kept at him, he suspected they were used to the air up here in Standing Rock.

He knew they were used to violating the regulations of the B.I.A. with white men, too. Although if Miss Polly's poor uncle had been getting any of this, he wouldn't have made such a damn fool of himself with kin.

He knew better than to warn either gal to be discreet about all this. He knew Indians didn't tattle much, anyway. While, if he pointed out that he was busting hell out of white man's law, they might consider it a hold on him. He was sated enough, now, to do some thinking as well as some screwing, and he knew he never should have started this, *if* he'd started it. It was hard to tell, coming in one pussy while playing with another.

Walking Willow shuddered in orgasm, fell off backward, and lay panting at the ceiling for a moment as her sister went on kissing him wildly, grabbing his now somewhat jaded tool as soon as she found it unoccupied. She said something in Lakota to her sister. Walking Willow giggled and said, "She says she wants to try something new."

"I feared she might, ma'am. Can I get my breath back first?"

"You don't have to do anything. *We'll* do it," his translator replied firmly. So he just lay there, firm as *he* could manage, while the two Indian gals worked out their new position atop him.

It was sort of unusual. Walking Willow lay against his chest, in the loving-up position, and took his organ grinder in hand to guide it as her sister climbed into place, facing the foot of the bed, to lower her moonlit brown rump as Walking Willow fondled it hard and aimed it up between her buttocks. As he felt where they were trying to fit it, he said, "A little further south, Miss Walking Willow. I fear you have it aimed at the wrong entrance."

But Walking Willow said, "She wants to take it in the rear hole. She says she has heard you men all like to do it that way to Pretty Blankets, and she wants to see if she's as good that way."

He gasped and said, "I'm sure she is, ma'am!" as Cherry Basket's tight anal opening slid down the length of his love-slicked shaft like a tight rubber band. She groaned and said something in Lakota that sounded dirty.

Her sister giggled but didn't translate as she kissed Longarm and moved his free hand down between her thighs. As he started massaging her clit while her sister screwed herself silly on his newly inspired erection, Walking Willow reached around with her own hand to play with her sister's clit and empty front opening. She was in a better position to do so, and it was nice to see that they felt no rivalry, after all.

The three of them went crazy until everyone concerned had come at least once more. Then Walking Willow announced a new round of musical crotch, in Lakota, so Longarm was a mite confused but went along with them as the good sport he was. He didn't ask the gals if Miss Pretty Blankets always did it this way, or mayhaps old-fashioned once in a while just to be different. He grinned as he considered the possibilities of having that long, skinny gal in the middle of this orgy with the two smaller and prettier sisters. It sure was funny how things that sounded a mite distasteful in the cold gray light of common sense seemed only good clean fun, once a man was *at* life down and dirty! He pictured the plump round rump he was abusing as leaner and bonier and it kept him going. He'd had so much this evening that he knew he was past lust into bragging, but he couldn't help wondering what it would be like to swap spit with a sort of ugly, long-nosed gal whilst laying a pretty one, and vice versa. It got him even hotter to consider pretty little blonde Polly in the same bed with tall, dark, homely Pretty Blankets, even though he knew *that* was pure fantasy. But, between the daydreaming and the changes of pace and partners, he managed to calm both the Falling Sky sisters down, screw 'em each old-fashioned one last time, and send 'em home satisfied.

As he lay there smoking, sure, now, that he'd never ride any goddamned anything far enough to matter in the near future, he wondered if the slap and tickle he'd just enjoyed bound him to checking out the missing sister, Dancing Antelope. He figured he owed it to the sweet little gals at least to check it out. And, hell, if the eldest sister was at all like her younger ones, he likely owed to himself as well.

Chapter 6

Neither the agent and his woman nor Polly's uncle had turned up the next morning. So Longarm walked over to the police station and borrowed a buckskin and a paint from Big Bear. They were both mares and of course unshod. But the buckskin didn't fuss about the army bridle and McClellan saddle as Big Bear held the horsehair lead of the paint for him. The Crow looked a mite disappointed as Longarm mounted, from the right instead of the left. "I see you've ridden our ponies before," he said.

Longarm laughed, took the lead line, and said, "Sorry to spoil your fun, old son, but it's tedious getting bucked off so early in the day. If I can't find someone to get these critters back to you, I'll put through a government voucher saying you sold 'em to me for forty each."

"That's a handsome price for an Indian pony, Longarm."

"That's what I just said. I got a favor to ask of you, too. Has it occurred to you that the agency folk have been gone long enough to have done anything sensible they had to do down at the other agency by now?"

"Yes. I've been wondering why they haven't come back after all this time. Do you think something could have happened to them?"

"Don't know. Can't tell, with the telegraph out. As you may have noticed, I can only move in one direction at a time. So while I ride off to send me some wires, catch me a train, or whatever, I'd like you to ride south and see if you can cut their trail. McLoughlin's a good thirty and mostly spacious miles. If something took out two armed men and mayhaps a tolerable tough woman, you won't want to meet up with it alone. You'd best deputize some backup."

The Crow frowned up at him and demanded, "How? B.I.A. regulations call for a full police detail here—but, as you see, I'm all alone! I can't get one damned Sioux to tell me the right time!"

Longarm shrugged. "Start packing your own watch and tell *them* what time it is, then. Go talk to White Bull and tell him to give you some of his young men."

"He won't like it, Longarm."

Longarm looked disgusted. "Now where in the U. S. Constitution does it say anyone has to *like* the law to obey it? The law gives any peace officer caught shorthanded the right to deputize himself a *posse comitatus,* and you are the local law, right?"

"It's not the same. White Bull has to obey you because you are a Meneaska. I am an Indian from an enemy nation."

Longarm frowned down at him and said, "What are you wearing that badge for, if you ain't man enough to back its medicine? You're supposed to be a federal officer. As to you being a Crow, it's tough shit if Lakota don't like taking orders from a Crow. The Lakota Nation got licked fair and square by the U. S. Cavalry and its Crow scouts. So stop acting like an infernal *loser,* Big Bear! Just tell White Bull you need his help, and if he tries to give you sass, lay down the *law* to him!"

The Crow still looked unconvinced, so Longarm added, "What's the matter, sonny? Do you need a white man to come along and hold your little hand while you looks another red man in the eye?"

That lit a fire under him. Big Bear started hopping about like a little kid trying not to piss his pants. "I wish that pony had thrown you!" he shouted. "I wish that pony had thrown you and shit on your head!"

He pounded his chest with a fist and added, "Hear me! I am Mahto-Tonka! I have counted coup on Sioux, and I am the *law* here! I don't need anyone to back my medicine! When I tell them what to do, I think they had better *do* it!"

Longarm chuckled, said he'd just said that, and rode off on the buckskin, leading the paint.

He'd had only a cup of awful trade coffee for breakfast and it seemed a mite rude to ride off without seeing how Miss Polly felt the morning after. But he'd learned the hard way that women had a limited number of ways to greet a man who'd made love to them, once they'd had time to cool down, and he didn't have time to listen to any of them. So he rode off across the prairie to the northwest, loping the ponies to settle both them and his stomach a mite.

It was a crisp sunny morning and the sun and prairie winds had baked the sod firm again by now. So the travel was easy on man and beast alike. The buffalo grass had taken advantage of that unexpected wet spell to grow an extra inch before drying out to standing straw again. He knew Big Bear would have a chore, now, cutting sign.

The High Plains rolled some in these parts, as if to justify how some folk called them "the sea of grass." Longarm had read someplace that once upon a time there *had* rolled a real sea here. That was why sometimes a seashell fell out of a drywash bank to startle folk camped so far from any recent ocean. He topped a rise, reined in, and turned in the saddle to gaze back with a frown at the Indian riding after him and shouting.

It was Miss Pretty Blankets. He grimaced as he compared his fantasy of the night before with the real thing in the harsh morning sunlight.

Pretty Blankets fell in beside him. "I have just been talking with those naughty Falling Sky girls."

Longarm heeled the buckskin into motion again as he replied. "It's a free country, I reckon. I'm riding off the reservation, Miss Pretty Blankets. It's been nice meeting up with you again, but..."

"I know where you are going," Pretty Blankets insisted, riding along on his left. "You are wasting your time. I know what happened to Dancing Antelope. She has run away for good this time. This time she was very bad. She stole from her own people instead of the trading post."

"Do tell? What are you missing, Miss Pretty Blankets?"

Pretty Blankets giggled. "She didn't steal anything from us girls. She broke into the shed where the old ones of the Strong Heart Society keep their medicine. She took the fox totem, some medicine bags, and other treasures of the Strong Hearts! Wakan Tonka knows *what* the elders will do to her if they ever see her again. Since my people have been confined and forbidden to follow the old ways, they will never be able to replace some of the ceremonial things that wicked girl has stolen."

Longarm whistled softly. "I heard she had taking ways, but stealing medicine is really pushing one's luck. Why do you figure she'd do such a fool thing, Miss Pretty Blankets?"

Pretty Blankets said, "She has been selling such things to a crazy woman of your people in Middle Fork. I don't know why the crazy Meneaska woman wants them, but she does, and she pays well for what she calls Indian art. Dancing Antelope has already sold her other things, but not sacred things. Dancing Antelope was very wicked to break into the treasure lodge of the Strong Hearts!"

Longarm nodded in agreement. "That's for damn sure. I thank you for telling me about it, Miss Pretty Blankets. You may have saved me some fruitless investigation."

"Good. Let's go back to my place and fuck."

He laughed incredulously. "Do you always phrase things so delicate, ma'am?" he asked.

"What's the matter? Don't you want me? You had those other girls, didn't you?"

He looked away. "That's for them to say, Miss Pretty Blankets."

Pretty Blankets tittered and said, "They already did. They say you are hung like a horse, and that you shoved it up both their rears. Come with me, good-looking, and I will show you an ass that really *likes* it!"

He felt his ears blushing as he kept riding on, saying, "That's a mighty tempting offer, Miss Pretty Blankets, but I ain't got time."

"All right. Why don't we just do it here? We're out of sight of the agency now."

"Uh, thanks, but no thanks, ma'am. I'm really in a hurry and, to tell you the truth, not feeling all that horny this morning for some reason."

"Let me suck you. That will put you in the mood, I'll bet!"

"It probably would, Miss Pretty Blankets." He laughed, picturing that long hooked nose rubbing in his pubic hair, but finding the picture less than inspiring. "Mayhaps when I ride back this way again, I'll take you up on your kind offer," he added. "But, somehow, I feel we'd get along better in the dark."

"Is that a promise, handsome one?"

He answered with a lewd smile and a sassy wink. Then heeled his mount into a lope and rode off fast, leading the paint and leaving Pretty Blankets in their dust.

An hour or more later, wide awake and having had the McClellan rub his balls awake, too, he wondered why he'd acted so shy back there.

He told the buckskin, "I must be getting old. For I've played slap and tickle with uglier gals in my time, and last night, with a hard-on, I was entertaining mighty dirty thoughts about Miss Pretty Blankets. But when she offered that skinny brown ass in broad day, it just didn't seem as appealing. Ain't human nature strange?"

The mare, being she-male as well as a dumb brute, had no idea what he was talking about, of course, so he shut up and rode on until, a few hours later, they got to the reservation's unfenced border along Cedar Creek. The creek looked more like a trickle of piss down a sandy dry wash in dry weather.

Longarm crossed over to White Man's Range. He dismounted and saddled the paint with the McClellan to ride on, fresh, leading the buckskin. It was just as tedious on the far side of Ceder Creek for a spell. Then he spied a sunflower windmill on the horizon and took a bearing on it. Riding toward the windmill got tedious, too, before they got close enough to matter. For the thin, dry air of the High Plains made things look a lot closer than they really were. But he finally topped a rise to see a quarter-section homestead laid out inside a bobwire fence. The nesters had planted a kitchen garden in the bared plot left when they'd cut the sods for the house. Another forty acres had been drilled for what looked like barley from here. Longarm didn't care what the nesters were trying to grow. He wanted water for his brutes and any information they might have on lost, strayed, or stolen Indian gals.

As he rode in, the front door of the soddy opened and a little old lady dressed in rusty black and packing a double-barreled twelve-gauge popped out like a cuckoo and proceeded to act as strange.

A skinny, younger gal in black ran out after her, shouting, "No, Granny, don't!" as the old lady aimed the scattergun at Longarm and pulled both triggers!

He was out of range for number nine buck, so he came off better than the old lady when the recoil of both barrels set her on her ass in the dust.

The considerable sound of the double blast spooked his mount a mite, but Longarm calmed the paint. As he saw that the younger gal had the empty twelve-gauge now, he rode in, ticking the brim of his Stetson as he called out, "I come in peace, ladies. My name is Custis Long and I'm a deputy U. S. marshal, so please don't shoot at me no more."

As her granddaughter helped her up, the old woman cried, "Keep away from us, you infernal savage! Our barley's just bouncing back from the awful way you and yourn mistreated it and, by gum, I'll have the law on you if you don't ride around, this time!"

The younger gal holding her and the shotgun shook her head. "Granny, the man just said he *is* the law!"

The old woman peered up at Longarm and croaked, "Oh, why didn't somebody say as much, then? You know I don't see good since I busted my specs, Sue Ann. I thought he was one of them savages, coming at us some more."

Longarm figured it was safe to dismount now. "What sort of savages are we talking about, ladies?" he asked. "Have you had Indian trouble this summer?"

The younger one shook her head, sunbonnet and all. "No," she said. "We treats the Sioux neighborly and they repays in kind. Granny's vexed about them *Rooshins* as has moved on to the range. They act like they own the whole country. Why, the other day, a couple of 'em rode smack across our barley without so much as a thank you, ma'am!"

Longarm frowned. "Russians? In Dakota? Riding over planted crops?" he asked incredulously.

Sue Ann nodded and explained. "They jumped the fence.

I reckon they considered it a sporting dare. They're always up to show-off stunts like that. Rooshins think they're the greatest aboard a bronc. But, if you ask me, they rides like show-off dudes!"

"They rides like Chinamen, and drunk ones at that," Granny said. "Come in the house and let us coffee and cake you, boy. If you're the law, I want to swear out a trespassing warrant on them infernal Rooshins!"

Longarm said something about watering his ponies first, but Sue Ann said she'd be proud to do it for him, and insisted he follow the old gal in. So he did. The interior walls of the soddy had been papered with newsprint and the dirt floor was neatly swept. Granny sat him at a plank table and proceeded to fill him with real Arbuckle and some mighty fine layer cake as she explained how she and her recently widowed grand-daughter were trying to hang on to the claim filed by the late man of the house. Longarm asked what had happened to him and learned once again that riding at a full gallop across a prairie-dog town could be injurious to one's health.

Sue Ann came in and took off her sunbonnet as Longarm expressed his sympathy. She turned out to be neither good-looking nor ugly, hatless. Her hair was straight and dish-water blonde. Her thin, pale face looked tired. Her figure was neither more nor less inspiring than that of old Pretty Blankets. It didn't matter; he wasn't figuring on staying long.

But their odd tale of Russian cavalry riding down their barley had aroused his interest. So he asked the woman to tell him all they knew about it, adding, "I'm interested in particular in how they're dressed. I got another complaint about rude Russians, it now seems, from another sort of U. S. citizen."

Sue Ann said, "Oh, you know how Rooshins dude themselves up, Deputy Long. They wears funny fur hats and long gray coats with rifle rounds pasted to their chests. I think they're Rooshin cook-shacks. That's what a cowboy passing called 'em. Cook-shacks."

"Cowboys and Injuns has tolerable manners, next to Rooshin cook-shacks, damn it!" Granny said.

Longarm washed down some cake with coffee. "I think the word is cossack, Ladies," he said. "Though I'll be blamed if I can figure what a Russian cossack or more was doing in your barley field or even in this neck of the woods. But you and an Indian lady must be telling me true, for you couldn't have both had the same funny dream. Have any of these whatevers tried to act forward with you, personal, Miss Sue Ann? I ain't just being nosy. I got a reason for asking."

The nester gal shook her head. "I stay indoors when I see any strange gent on the skyline, if I can. None of them has ever come up to the door. They just rides by like the wind, singing or laughing like idjets in their own funny lingo. That cowboy says they're off a spread, a big spread, up near Middle Fork."

Granny scowled and said darkly, "They're overdue for some night riding, I vow! They got no manners at all, and the folks about Middle Fork has had just about enough of the rascals by now!"

Longarm said firmly, "It's best to leave untidy neighbors to the law, these days, Granny. The time for vigilance committees has more than passed. It's downright illegal nowadays."

Granny snorted. "A lot you know, boy! Lots of folk has already swore out complaints agin them infernal cook-shacks, and the law ain't done a thing to cook-shack one!"

He nodded understandingly. "I'll talk to the law when I reach Middle Fork, Granny. There's one gent dressed cossack I mean to question particular about his manners. But let me ask you about something else. I'm trying to cut the trail of a Lakota gal called Dancing Antelope, and —"

"Oh, *her*," Sue Ann cut in. "We don't let her stop for water here no more. Not since she tried to steal Granny's sewing basket."

"Then you know her?" he asked.

"Not now. Did. She's a sneak thief and some say worse. I would tell you what I heard she does for randy white men on considerable occasion if we were married or at least engaged. But since we ain't, you'll just have to figure it out yourself, sir!"

He grimaced and said, "Don't have to. Others less shy have already told me she's sort of wayward. But she's still a ward of the U. S. A., and she's missing. Do you ladies recall when Dancing Antelope last came by your spread?"

Neither white woman could, so Longarm thanked them for their hospitable manners and rose to leave. Sue Ann followed him outside. When they were alone, she asked if he'd be coming by again soon. He said he didn't know. "I sort of wish you'd try," she said. "Granny's a mighty sound sleeper, and—well, I loves her, but she ain't much company."

He said he followed her drift, told he he'd keep her offer in mind, and changed saddles to ride out on the buck again, leading the paint. As soon as they were alone on the prairie again he laughed and said, "Jesus, if that don't beat all. How is it a man can spend a whole infernal week in a big town like Denver, missing every brass ring he tries to kiss, and then, just as he's in a hurry in the middle of nowheres, gals start leaping out at him from every damned direction?"

He lit a cheroot and added, "And how is it that gals who talk dirty about other gals are always the first to leap at a poor innocent cuss?"

He decided the skinny dishwater widow was likely jealous of the missing Indian gal. That likely meant she was as pretty as, or prettier than, her two bawdy kid sisters. He was kind of looking foward to finding her. He didn't have anything much worth stealing and found the Falling Sky sisters mighty good company. He wondered if Dancing Antelope was as light-skinned as Walking Willow. He'd noticed she'd had a paler hide and more European features than old Pretty Blankets. The Falling Sky sisters likely had at least one captive white gal on their family tree.

The was something more lawful to study on. If Dancing Antelope had run away to try and live off the blanket, it seemed unlikely anyone would ever find out just what had happened to her. She'd have sold the stolen medicine objects by now, if nobody had stolen *her*. Dressed white and packing money, a light-skinned Lakota gal who spoke tolerable English could easily pass herself off as a Mexican or a free breed.

He shrugged and heeled his mount into a steady lope. Billy Vail hadn't sent him up here to look for wayward gals or even mysterious Russian cossacks. He'd mention both to the law in Middle Fork and let them deal with local problems after he wired the office and found out if it was all right to head back, now that he'd done all he'd been told to up here. Billy Vail had told him not to chase after side issues, and this time he meant to follow instructions for a change.

He would have, too, if some other folk in North Dakota had been sensible enough to behave until Longarm could ride out.

Chapter 7

Middle Fork looked like just what it was, a bitty trail town in the middle of nowhere. It took its name and its reason for being from the Middle Fork Wash, a sometimes stream running uncertainly south into the more imposing depths of Cedar Creek, now a long day's ride behind him. Longarm and the ponies were trail weary as they rode in near sundown. Longarm bedded Paint and Buck in the town livery with plenty of water and oats. He was thirsty and hungry himself, but he went to the local Western Union office first.

He greeted the lone clerk on duty and picked up a pad of telegraph blanks and a pencil stub to wire his office the news of his arrival. He told his boss White Bull had said just what they'd figured in Denver he would say. He didn't mention cossacks or missing Indian gals. He doubted Billy Vail would be interested in either.

When he handed the message over and told the clerk to send it collect, the Western Union man said, "If you're Deputy Long, I have a message for you as well. It came in just a little while ago."

He handed Longarm the yellow sheet. Longarm took it with a frown. He knew Billy Vail was a slick old lawman, but he hadn't planned on showing up in Middle Fork and never would have, had the wire at the agency been open.

The wire wasn't from Denver. It was from the Indian agency at McLaughlin. It read:

BIG BEAR AND SIOUX POSSE JUST ARRIVED STOP THEY SAY THEY WERE LOOKING FOR AGENT KRUGER HIS WIFE AND TRADER BEAN FROM OTHER AGENCY BUT FOUND NO SIGN STOP WHAT IS GOING ON QUESTION MARK NONE OF THOSE PEOPLE WERE EXPECTED HERE STOP SIGNED LOGAN SIOUX AGENT MCLAUGHLIN

Longarm folded the message and put it away with a thoughtful frown. Then he asked for his wire to Vail back and added:

SOMEONE SEEMS TO BE VANISHING FOLK OFF STANDING ROCK RESERVATION STOP WE ARE MISSING TWO WHITE MEN ONE WHITE WOMAN ONE INDIAN GAL STOP AWAITING INSTRUCTIONS

Then, having done his duty to his job, Longarm left to do his duty to his stomach. A rinky-tink piano up the street told him of a saloon that would certainly be serving free snacks as well as beer at this hour. He strode up the plank walk, parted the batwing doors, and, sure enough, a buffet of cold meats, sliced cheese, and such was down the bar near the piano. Since the professor seated at the piano wasn't eating any of it, Longarm went down and proceeded to build himself a heroic sandwich.

The bartender slid down his way, regarding Longarm with morose concern until the tall deputy said, "Don't get

71

your bowels in an uproar. I'm drinking, too. I'd like a boilermaker. Maryland Rye, if you got it."

The bartender nodded and proceeded to put the makings between them on the mahogany. But he held on to the bottle and beer schooner until Longarm put a silver cartwheel down, asking, "What makes you such a trusting soul?"

The bartender shrugged. "A long hard life, pilgrim. No offense, but you're a total stranger, and dressed like a dusty indeed gambling man. I hope you have the forethought to consult the local law about our fair city's ordinances before you set up your faro layout. Our sheriff is sort of testy."

Longarm laughed. "I thank you for the compliment about my looks. I have to dress sissy because I ride for the U. S. A. As to your sheriff's feelings, I mean to pay a courtesy call on him, once I recover from some serious riding."

Longarm commenced wolfing down the grub and beverage. The bartender moved off to serve other customers. The saloon was starting to fill as the dulcet tones of the rinky-tink piano lured passersby in out of the hot sunset.

Longarm had just finished his sandwich and was considering another when the batwing doors parted to let Hard-Ass Henry Harrison in. Longarm had never met Hard-Ass Henry in the flesh before, but he knew him well from the many plaintive posters describing his disregard for other people's lives and property. Longarm quietly put down the beer schooner and casually unbuttoned his frock coat as the big, ugly outlaw strode his way with a jingle of spurs and a silver-mounted S&W .45 riding each hip.

Longarm was still considering how best to break the news that Hard-Ass Henry was under arrest when their eyes met. The outlaw blanched and went for both guns at once.

Longarm beat him to the draw—just—and everyone but Hard-Ass Henry dove for cover as Longarm's double-action .44 informed the desperado that slapping leather on a man who'd seen you first was not a good move.

Hard-Ass Henry rolled off down the bar, taking round after round in his thick trunk, until he finally wound up flat on his back on the sawdust-covered floor, staring wistfully up at the pressed tin ceiling. He moaned, "Oh, hell, what's a pro like Longarm doing in such a pissy little trail town?"

Longarm had one round left in his sixgun, so he stepped over to kick the outlaw's own guns clear of the dying man's reach. "I'm sorry somebody described me so well to you, Hard-Ass Henry. I would have taken you less noisy, had I been able."

The man at his feet sighed and said, "I wouldn't have gone with you quiet in any case, pard. This way can't be worse than hanging. How did you trail me here, Longarm? Nobody was supposed to know I was anywheres near the Dakotas."

"I reckon you've become too famous to pass anywhere incognito, Hard-Ass Henry," said Longarm, turning to the assemblage in the saloon to add, "I sure wish somebody would go get a doc."

A couple of men headed for the door. But the man on the floor laughed weakly. "It's too late for a doc, Longarm. You've done me good, and for that, at least, I thanks you. A boy gets tired of running, and I sure didn't want to dance my last dance at the end of that rope!"

Longarm nodded soberly. "I thank *you* for being such a good sport, Hard-Ass Henry. I'd buy you a drink on it, but I dunno, the way I hulled your innards, it might not set too well."

The dying outlaw didn't answer. He couldn't. Longarm started reloading as he told the dead man, "Damn it, I was hoping we could clear up that little matter of the U. P. mail car last month. But since everyone says it was you, we'll just say no more about it."

A man wearing a brass star and a drawn sixgun charged in. Longarm quickly lowered his own gun to his side. "I'm law," he said, before either of them could get in trouble. The older lawman nodded but kept his own gun in hand until Longarm had flashed his federal badge. Then he put his own gun away and said, "I'm Sheriff Lansford. What have we here on the floor?"

"I'm U. S. Deputy Marshal Custis Long, and this here used to be Hard-Ass Henry Harrison," Longarm said. "He's wanted for crimes too numerous to mention and was last seen over by the South Pass, stopping trains for a living. If you want the paperwork, the reward on him is considerable, and I ain't allowed to collect bounties, damn it."

That seemed to put the sheriff in a mighty friendly mood. So after the boys carried Hard-Ass Henry's remains off to the undertaker's, the two lawmen bellied up to the bar to celebrate their new-found friendship.

As they compared notes, Longarm learned that Lansford had lead the posse that found the body of the Kiowa Kid. He was too polite to inquire just who in hell had elected Lansford sheriff in what seemed to be a still unincorporated county. Things tended to be run a mite informally in territories that hadn't made statehood yet.

That reminded Longarm of vigilante talk, so he asked the old sheriff to tell him about the mysterious Russians he'd been hearing about.

Lansford swore. "Hell, son, there's no mystery about it. A Russian prince named Deltorsky, André Deltorsky, I think, has set his fool self up as a cattle baron just north of here, over the Cannonball Divide. He's rich as hell, as well as crazy. He's got the closest thing to a castle you can build outten sod, and way more cows than the good Lord ever intended for dry Dakota range. Them cossacks pestering everyone works for him. They don't just work for him. He *owns* 'em. He inherited a whole tribe of the crazy Russian

74

cusses from his daddy, it seems. They is what you call serfs in Russia."

Longarm signaled the bartender for another round as he frowned and said, "I may be wrong. I've hardly ever been to Russia, but it seems to me I read somewheres that a recent Czar set all them serfs free. It was just about the time Abe Lincoln did as much for the slaves over here. So there ain't been no serfs in Russia for a spell."

Lansford shrugged. "Maybe they don't read the same papers as you," he said. "Maybe they don't *mind* being owned by a prince. You know how some darkies stayed on to work the same plantation after the War. Whatever them cossacks are, they're a pure pain in the ass. They don't know how to talk American, or how to act American. They just swagger about in them funny hats like they think *we* must be serfs, too!"

"I heard as much from a Lakota gal called Pretty Blankets and some nester women I met up with today," Longarm said. "How come you let them act so disgusting? Can't you gather a big enough posse to handle one outfit, big or not?"

Sheriff Lansford swore and said, "Shit, I could take 'em all on by myself, if my hands wasn't tied, boy! I've talked myself blue in the face at them Russian rascals. But Prince Deltorsky has what they call diplomas of immunity."

Longarm frowned. "Diplomatic immunity? That don't make sense."

"That's what I just said," Lansford agreed, signaling for another round.

"To have diplomatic immunity, a cuss is supposed to be a diplomat," Longarm said. "Does the Russian Czar have a mission in Dakota?"

"Prince Deltorsky's only mission seems to be raising cows and hell. What difference do it make if the Czar is in on it or not?"

"I'd better send me some wires and find out. There's

75

something queer going on here. If this Russian prince is some kind of diplomat, what in the hell is he doing running a cattle spread? I thought you had to be a U. S. citizen to file a homestead claim. If he ain't filed proper for his water rights and home spread, he don't belong on them, acting right or not. If he *does* own land under U. S. law, the son of a bitch ought to be acting more neighborly."

The sheriff said, "It's a waste of time sending wires to Washington, son. I've already done so. They told me he's important at the Russian Court in Saint Pete's, so they gave him that diploma at the U. S. Embassy over there afore he come over here. As to the land he owns, he never filed no homestead claim. He bought it for hard cash offen an American who'd already proven his claim and should have been ashamed of hisself. I know it sounds dislawful, but lawyers tell me a gent packing one of them diplomas has a constitutional right to buy anything they wants."

Longarm nodded. "Diplomats are allowed to buy property to reside on, lest they wind up camped on the Mall in Washington. I know some foreign syndicates own cow spreads over here, too. But running any kind of business with diplomatic immunity would give any businessman advantages that *can't* be constitutional!"

A townee who'd been listening in on the far side of the sheriff chimed in. "Advantages, gents? Jesus Christ, if I could run my own business knowing nothing I did could get me arrested, I'd be able to dower my daughter with the Northern Pacific or mayhaps Western Union by the time she was old enough to marry off! I'd just start by telling every son of a bitch I owed money to that I had me this here diplomatic immunity and then, Powder River and let her buck!"

The sheriff laughed and introduced the townsman as Big Mike Maldan. Longarm shook and pretended not to hear when the sheriff added that the big bluff townee was a local contractor and a leader of the Middle Fork vigilance committee. It was Lansford's town. If he wanted to drink with folks he ought to be arresting, Longarm figured it wasn't a federal matter.

Big Mike said, "That goddamned Triangle Crown owes *me*, for the dozen wells I drilled for 'em months ago. You know what my lawyer tells me?"

"First back up and tell me what a Triangle Crown might be, Big Mike," Longarm said.

"That's the brand Prince Deltorsky registered in Bismarck. Ain't that silly? Anyways, the sassy Russian's sitting up on the high flats betwixt the drainage of the Cedar and the Cannonball, and as anyone but a Russian knows, Jesus don't need souls like cows need water out here during a dry spell. I sunk him a mess of right deep wells along the divide, and I've yet to be paid for the goddamn pipe, let alone my labor!"

The sheriff said, "I hear tell he's yet to pay for the windmills he ordered from Chicago to pump said water, too."

Big Mike nodded. "The son of a bitch ain't paid for nothing! He owes for everything from his fancy house to the cows grazing all about it, drinking the damn water I drilled for 'em! He don't even pay his help, I hear tell. That's likely why them hand of hissen ride about in them funny hats, stealing."

Longarm frowned thoughtfully and asked, "What have they been stealing, Big Mike?"

The contractor signaled for a round. "Anything as ain't nailed down," he replied sourly. "You never *seen* such rascals for stealing as them Russian cowhands."

The sheriff growled, "I got warrants out on everything from missing stock to a gal's sunbonnet. Damn fool Cossack ripped the hat right offen a nester gal's head as he rode by, for some fool reason. But they all looks alike and Bismarck says I can't lock any of the bastards up in any case!"

Big Mike said darkly, "Me and the boys have been studying on that. We must look a lot alike to them furriners, too. So who's to say who might or might not come calling some night with a feed sack over his head and a stick of sixty percent in his free hand?"

The sheriff snapped, "I didn't hear that, Big Mike! For God's sake, don't you know better than to discuss night riding in front of two growed lawmen?"

Big Mike just chuckled and hid his face in his beer suds for a spell.

"I didn't hear that, neither," Longarm said. "I can't do anything about civil disturbances or even local thieving. So let's get back to more serious matters. I'm missing me some folk the government has a fatherly interest in. Have any of them cossacks ever done anything really *ornery* to anyone you know of, Sheriff?"

Lansford shrugged. "Well, we heard a gal over on the Cannonball side of the divide was raped while her man was off the spread on business. I ain't sure if it really happened of if it's just one of them stories that drifts on the wind. When I asked for details, nobody could pin down no names or places."

Big Mike said, "It was likely one of them Russian cossacks. The only white man in these parts as ever raped gals regular was that Kiowa Kid, and he's under the sod for good, the son of a bitch."

Longarm politely repressed a yawn. He'd just ridden twice as far in one day as most men would have wanted to, and idle chatter about distant crimes that couldn't be substantiated were mighty tedious to a lawman even when he felt more chipper.

78

He said, "Speaking of the late Kiowa Kid, I'd sort of like a closer look at the arrow you found in his back, Sheriff. I couldn't tell much from a photograph. I hope you didn't bury it with him."

Lansford frowned thoughtfully. "Damned if I know, to tell the truth. We just sprayed the ants and wrapped the rascal in a tarp out on the prairie. Or, rather, the undertaker did. That's who'd know if the arrow's in his grave with him or not."

Longarm put down his half-filled schooner and said, "I'd best have a talk with him, then. He's likely open late anyway, right?"

Lansford chuckled. "That's for sure, since you just referred a customer to 'em. I'll show you the way. And by the way, said undertaker is a she, not a he."

As he led the way outside, the sheriff added thoughtfully, "Never have understood why a decent-looking little gal wanted to take up such a trade. But, come to think of it, I don't see why any *man* would want to be a corpse washer, neither."

Longarm agreed there was no accounting for human tastes as they moved up the walk together. It was really dark out now, but a light in the front window of the funeral parlor told them the place was still open, so they went in.

A bell fixed over the door announced their presence in the main room filled with hopefully empty caskets on display. The curtains hanging across a doorway leading back to more serious matters parted and a dark gal wearing a rubber apron over gray duds came out. The sheriff introduced her to Longarm as Miss Dorothy Dobbs. She peeled off a rubber glove to shake and said she'd be proud to show Longarm around. Sheriff Lansford said something about having to get home to supper and left, looking sort of unsettled.

The undertaking gal smiled wanly and said, "The smell of formaldehyde affects some people like that. I'm sorry. There's nothing I can do about it when I'm working. I tried burning incense at the same time and it even made *me* sick."

Longarm nodded. "I met Mister Death at Shiloh, ma'am, without no embalming fluid to disguise his breath."

She nodded and led the way back to where Hard-Ass Henry lay naked on a zinc-covered table, looking mighty pale. "I've noted the probable cause for the coroner's office, if they ever get around to asking for it," she said. "You're a pretty good shot, Deputy Long."

"Call me Custis. To tell you true, there's no mystery to me about the death of that gent on your table at the moment. I understand you had the delicate task of putting the Kiowa Kid in the ground, ma'am."

She grimaced and said, "I did. That job was a bit rich, even for my blood. It would have been a waste of time to embalm him, even if he hadn't been buried on the township at minimal rates. We just dropped him in the ground as he was."

"Arrow and all, ma'am?"

She shook her head. "No. I tried to neaten him up at least that much. I have it over here someplace, if you need it."

She turned and moved to a cupboard, opening a drawer with her back to him. She was built sort of nice. He wondered if she was spoken for, despite her odd occupation.

She turned around to hand him the Lakota arrow. He held it up to the light, noting its owl-feather fletching and red medicine stripes. He nodded. "It's the real thing, right enough. I see it even has one of them Hudson Bay trade heads the B.I.A. don't approve of these days. Them wicked barbs likely explain the arrow being left in the poor cuss. It's hard to draw a Hudson Bay head out without busting the shaft. I notice you managed, though."

She made a wry face and said, "By the time I tried it was easy enough. There wasn't much for those barbs to grip. Have you ever seen a dead cat left overlong to the blowflies in the sun and wind?"

He sighed. "You sure paint a pretty picture, ma'am. I'm glad I ate already. Though I had planned on something more substantial before I called it a day." He handed the arrow back. "I'd like you to keep this for me for now, Miss Dorothy. It won't fit in my pockets and I doubt I'll ever need it for evidence in any case."

She nodded, put the arrow away again, and asked how she'd find him if need be. He smiled ruefully. "I ain't sure. I still have to scout up a place to bed down for the night. I'll likely be leaving as soon as my office wires back that it's all right."

She looked sort of disappointed and asked him why he'd come all that way if he only meant to turn about and go back. So he explained his fool's errand, leaving out some of the dirty parts. He could see she found it a fool's errand, too, so he added, "Them folks who vanished off the reservation may or may not tie in somewhat with the late Kiowa Kid. But I'll be switched if I can figure how, Miss Dorothy."

She said, "Well, you do have an unsolved Indian killing over to the west and something mysterious going on at the reservation to the southeast."

"I do," he said, "but connecting them up is a chore. No other whites in these parts report even *seeing* a Lakota on or off the warpath this summer. The only Indians who've been off the reservation at all in this direction was both gals. And neither seems to have been out to lift anyone's scalps."

She repressed a smile. "I've heard the scandal about both those wayward squaws, Custis. I'd be very surprised if either

81

of them killed and scalped the Kiowa Kid."

"He likely would have been, too, ma'am. I doubt many women, red or white, could draw the bow as must have sent that heavy arrow so deep into his flesh. Besides that, Dancing Antelope and Pretty Blankets don't enjoy reputations for *disliking* white boys. If anything, they both seem to have been right friendly gals."

Dorothy laughed. "I said I'd heard. Dancing Antelope is the one who's missing, right?"

"So far. Miss Pretty Blankets tells me a gent who describes as sort of Russian trifled with her a few days ago, but she got away."

"Good heavens! Are you suggesting the other one might not have?"

"Don't know. Mean to ask them Russians come morning. Too late to ride out there tonight. Do you mind if I smoke, ma'am?"

"Not at all. I was hoping you were used to the smell by now," she said.

He waited until he'd fished out a cheroot and lit up before he said, "That ain't why I asked, ma'am. I said I've smelt worse things in my time. But if you don't mind my being nosy, I have been sort of wondering..."

She sighed. "Wondering how a nice girl like me wound up in a job like this? That's easy. I studied medicine back east. I graduated, too. But when it came time to apply for my license to practice medicine, they noticed I was a woman."

He nodded soberly. "I've noticed that, too, Miss Dorothy. I'm sorry some menfolk can be so mule-headed about gals taking jobs reserved for us big strong cusses. I take it you settled for caring for the dead when they wouldn't license you to care for the living?"

She nodded but spoke bitterly. "There's not as much

82

difference as one might think, given the present state of the medical arts. I was in debt for my education. This business was up for sale. So when I saw the advertisement, I did what I had to do."

He glanced approvingly at the cadaver of Hard-Ass Henry and said, "I can see you do it good, Miss Dorothy. Old Henry never looked half so decent before. But I'm keeping you from finishing your chores here. So I'd best be on my way."

She started to cover Hard-Ass Henry with a sheet as she replied. "Actually, I'm finished with the embalming, and we won't be dressing him until my assistants show up for work in the morning."

He nodded. "He would be a mite heavy for one gal to tussle with—no offense." He hesitated before going on. "I'm aiming to scout up some steak and potatoes, ma'am. I'd be proud to share 'em with you, if you ain't got nothing better to do."

She looked startled. "Are you asking me to have dinner with you, sir?" she asked.

"Only if you want it, ma'am. I ain't holding a gun on you."

She laughed. "I'm so glad. Those .44 rounds make such a task for mortician's wax. But where were you thinking of taking me? The only places open at this hour serve dreadful food. Most people in this small town eat at home, you see."

"I know only too well what they rustle up for passers-through they'll likely never see again in trail-town beaneries, ma'am," Longarm said. "But I don't have a home here to take you to, so—"

"We could do as well or better in my kitchen," she cut in, then added awkwardly, "Of course, if you have delicate feelings . . ."

He smiled down at her. "Don't you take off them rubber gloves before you fry a steak, Miss Dorothy?"

She laughed again. "You're on! Let's go. My place is out back, across the yard."

He waited until she'd locked up and doused the lamps before he followed her out the back door and across a well-tended garden to the frame cottage behind the undertaking establishment. He didn't ask her why she didn't live over the shop, like some. He knew fumes tended to rise.

Dorothy Dobbs kept her modest house the way she kept her hair and duds: neat and unpretentious. The four-room layout was familiar to him. A firm in Chicago sold such cottages by mail order, prefabricated. A big cast-iron heater formed the core with parlor, kitchen, bedroom, and indoor bath wrapped about the central open space. When the Wolf Wind blew down across the snow-covered prairie in January she likely left all the doors facing the heater open and the outside wall would still frost some.

She sat him at the kitchen table, poked up the fire in her cooking range, and excused herself to duck into her bath for a spell. He'd noticed she'd peeled off the rubber gloves and apron before leaving Hard-Ass Henry in the dark, but it cheered him just the same to hear her splashing lots of soap and water next door before they ate.

He'd about smoked his cheroot away entirely when she came back, wearing a fresh housedress and glowing from her wet hair down as if she'd been scrubbed with lye soap and sandpaper. He didn't comment on it as she proceeded to rustle them up some grub.

She said, "It would take less time if you liked your potatoes home fried," so he said that was fine with him and offered to help. She told him to just sit and that it would only take a jiffy. So he did, and she was right. She cooked as efficiently as she did her less appetizing chores. He admired the no-nonsense movements of her skilled hands. She dropped a brace of steaks in a monstrous skillet and asked if he liked his medium or rare. "Just injure the cow gravely, ma'am," he said, and she laughed and said she preferred hers rare, too. So in no time at all they were eating together.

Like most country-reared men, Longarm ate seriously, saving small talk for dessert. But she must have been sort of lonely, for she tended to chatter like a magpie starved for company as he just dug in. He replied with nods to most of her remarks. But when she got to the part about how few men fancied the company of an undertaking gal, he had to answer in words. "Some folks are like that, I reckon. They just don't like to think about what's down the road ahead of us all, sooner or later."

"It doesn't upset you to be having dinner with...well, a ghoul?"

"Hell, Miss Dorothy, you ain't no ghoul. You're just a handsome gal as happens to be in a ghoulish trade. I said some folks face Mister Death with more feelings than brains. Your job ain't no worse than any other meat cutter's. Folks who act nervous around you never stop to consider that the carcass of the cow they're having for supper was treated a lot more brutal than anyone who's ever passed through your hands. Right?"

She laughed, but said, "I think you just spoiled my appetite. But what you say is true, damn it. If I'd opened shop here as a butcher girl, I'd doubtless have all sorts of young men sparking me by now."

He chuckled. "No doubt about it. For, like I said, you're a right handsome little gal, Miss Dorothy. I find it hard to believe nobody here in Middle Fork has noticed you friendly, considering the way some have violated federal law with wards of the Indian agency of late."

She wrinkled her pretty nose and said, "I'm not sure if

I should take that as a gallant compliment or an insult. Are you comparing me to a Sioux whore, sir?"

"Call me Custis. I likely should have chosen my words more careful. I only meant you are prettier than your average Lakota gal, to a white man, leastways. As to the morals of other ladies, you have to understand that Indians ain't more or less well-behaved than we are. They just look at things different."

"Do you call selling yourself for a bottle of firewater proper?"

"I just said I call it *different,* ma'am. Few Indians went to finishing school. So some of their habits may seem a mite disorderly to us. On the other hand, most Indians are shocked dreadful by manners most white folk admire. They think it's awful that nine-year-old white kids are working in cotton mills back East as we sit here feeling better than Indians. They have some surly comment to offer on the way some government officials keep their word as well. But rehashing busted treaties is too tedious to go into, so we'll say no more about 'em. You sure fry a fine steak, Miss Dorothy."

She said she could do better than that and when she served the coffee and peach cobbler she'd baked he saw she spoke with a straight tongue.

Longarm was enjoying her company and didn't want to leave. But a man could only put away so many helpings and he still didn't know where he'd be spending the rest of the night. If all else failed, he supposed he could unroll his bedroll in the hayloft above his stabled ponies.

She must have enjoyed his company, too. When he shoved his plate away with a contented sigh she rose and led him into the parlor instead of to the door. So they wound up sitting side by side on her horsehair sofa as she served what she called after-dinner brandy. It tasted like plain old brandy to Longarm, but it sure did loosen her up some. With one

86

thing and another they wound up with her sort of snuggled against him on the sofa as she went on complaining about how lonesome life was out here for an undertaking gal.

He couldn't smoke in this position, lest he set her brunette hair on fire, and he was getting tired of uttering soothing words as she spilled her hurt on his shoulder. So he kissed her instead.

Dorothy stiffened in his arms at first, then kissed back with considerable warmth. But, being a woman, when they came up for air she had to ask why he'd done such a forward thing.

He went on holding her, albeit loose enough to avoid spooking her, as he replied soberly, "You're right. It's getting late and I ought to be studying on shelter for the night instead of insulting ladies."

"I don't feel insulted," she said. "Just confused. It's been so long since any man kissed me, Custis."

So he kissed her again, and this time put a little more warmth into the effort as she responded in kind. It was her idea to start tonguing. He figured it was only polite to return the compliment by cupping a breast in his free hand, and when she didn't flinch at that, he just naturally slipped the hand inside the somehow unbuttoned front of her bodice to tease her turgid nipple right.

That made her roll her lips from his to murmur, "If we don't stop, I fear there's no question where you'll be spending the night, Custis. But are you sure you . . . want me?"

He laughed. "Hell, no, you're ugly as sin and I'd much rather sleep with a horse." Then since the conversation was getting so silly, he kissed her some more to shut her up as he started moving the hand down inside her housedress, across her warm flesh. He'd suspected she hadn't put on any underwear when she'd leaped from that quick bath before supper.

She must have liked what he was doing, for she didn't

resist. But as he parted the dark fuzz between her thighs with his exploratory fingers she pulled away and said, "Not here on the sofa, darling. Please stop teasing me, if you really want to."

He picked her up and walked into the bedroom with her, blessing the mail-order house for laying out their cottages so regular. He lowered Dorothy to the big brass bedstead. The bedsprings were noisy as hell, but who else was listening as they tore off the first ice-breaker half dressed? He made her come—it was easy—before rolling off to undress them both as she moaned and groaned about how she'd never meant it to go this far, but how lonely she'd been, and so on. Then, once he had her properly shucked, she climbed on top and proceeded to screw him silly.

He admired the way the light from the doorway outlined her shapely torso as she bounced up and down on him, her perky breasts bouncing the other way until he hauled her down closer and started kissing them. She giggled and said his moustache tickled. Then she moaned and added, "Oh, Lord, you're not tickling me now between my thighs! I didn't know men came this big, and—Jesus, I'm coming again, too!"

He rolled her over and got on top to finish right. He decided, when Dorothy raised her legs and hooked her bare toes in the brass above their heads, that it was mighty unlikely he was abusing a virgin.

That eased his mind. He felt sorry for any lonely gal, but he'd gotten into this without considering the cold gray dawn and, while her position in the community didn't bother him much, he wasn't planning on staying long. It seemed mean to treat such a nice little gal lightly.

He braced himself on locked elbows to gaze down at the view as he moved in and out of her in such a welcoming position. He decided he'd hardly be likely to meet anything prettier in Middle Fork, and anyone who screwed better would likely be the death of him. So he figured they might as well go steady, for now, at least.

He came in her, hard. She must have wanted to keep him hard, because when he rolled off to get his second wind she climbed back aboard him and started kissing her way down his heaving chest and naked belly as she forked a leg over to sort of sit on his face. He knew she'd just had a bath and that, experienced as she had to be, she hadn't been with another gent in recent memory. So, as she started giving him a French lesson, he figured it was only polite to tongue her clit as he ran two fingers in and out of her quivering little love box.

By the time he had the love-starved undertaking gal calmed down enough to think straight, they'd come together French, Greek, and a couple of ways he would have said were impossible had not she insisted on at least trying them. But nothing lasts forever, no matter how good it might feel. So they finally wound up side by side on the considerably rumpled sheets with a fresh cheroot in Longarm's teeth and Dorothy's adoring head on his naked shoulder.

She said, "Good heavens, I can't believe we did some of the things we just did, Custis. You must think I'm a slut!"

He patted her naked rump fondly. "Don't start talking dirty just because you've cooled a mite, honey. You didn't suggest nothing I wasn't willing to try, and I don't feel dirty."

"But I let you—I begged you to commit crimes against nature!"

"Oh, hell, girl, let nature worry about herself. If it didn't feel good, nobody would do it, so where's the crime?"

She giggled. "You're just awful. Isn't there anything that shocks you, Custis?"

"Sure. I don't hold with killing, stealing, or breaking one's given word. A banker dude evicting a family shocks me beyond words. As a lawman I run across all sorts of shocking behavior. But what a man and woman might or might not do in bed together, willing, strikes me as good clean fun."

She fondled his semi-erection as she purred, "I'm looking forward to you recovering your strength, darling. But I must say I find your attitude somewhat confusing. You obviously consider anything a man can do to a woman a harmless pastime. Yet you're worried about whether a cheap Sioux slut has been raped or not."

He grimaced and said, "They like to be called Lakota and valued as human beings, honey. The key word is *willing*. I don't hold with even winking at a gal if she don't *want* you to! The crime of rape has little to do with who's shoving what into whom. Rape is a crime because it's criminal for anyone to force anyone else to do anything they don't want to. Indians is wards of the federal government. It's my job to arrest anyone as bothers 'em in any way. So it don't matter if some rascal raped Miss Dancing Antelope or stole her blankets. It ain't allowed to mistreat an unwilling person, red or white, in any way. Besides, if she'd only been raped, we'd have heard from her by now. So what happened could be more serious."

He blew a thoughtful smoke ring and added, "While we're on the subject, and seeing as you'd likely know from experience, how far would you say the smell of a dead gal might carry on the wind at this time of the year?"

She shuddered and gasped, "Good God, what a topic for bedtime conversation! You may find this hard to believe, darling, but I really don't enjoy shop talk at romantic times like this."

He insisted, "Hell, we got to talk about *something* while I get my second wind, and you're an expert on the subject whose word carries weight with me. I figure since the open range ain't deserted entire, with cowhands and such riding hither and yon across it, a dead gal would have been discovered by now, if she was just lying there on the prairie, right?"

Dorothy played with his tool absently as she said thoughtfully, "Well, it's gotten dry again. But if that missing Indian girl lies somewhere in the open, nobody's ridden within a quarter mile of her remains, downwind. An observant rider who knows the country would have noticed hovering carrion crows from an even greater distance, don't you imagine?"

"I do. I figure she has to be under the sod or inside some building, dead or alive. I doubt she could be shacked up here in Middle Fork without the sheriff noticing. But I heard she was in the habit of selling Indian relics to some white lady here in town, Dorothy. Would you have any notion as to who that might be?"

She snuggled closer as she said, "It sounds like Mabel Parkman, the minister's wife, up the street at the First Church of Salvation. They're the only church in town who'll allow us to use their burial ground for scamps like the Kiowa Kid and that other gentleman you shot this evening. I think she does collect Indian junk. I've never been invited in after services."

He made a mental note to check out the First Church of Salvation come morning. Meanwhile, Dorothy had inspired him to new heights. So he snubbed out his smoke, rolled aboard, and as her lush wet warmth enveloped him once more, forgot all about the missing folk and where they might or might not have gone. For, at the moment, he was more interested in coming.

Dorothy must have grasped his intent as well as his shaft. She raised her astoundingly limber limbs to cross her trim ankles atop his head and seemed to be trying to crack his skull like a nut in a cracker as the bedsprings creaked loudly.

Chapter 8

Parting was such sweet sorrow it was often a pain in the ass. So when Longarm woke up at dawn to learn Dorothy snored he eased out of bed without waking her, sneaked his duds on, and let himself out. As he found the back gate in the cold gray light he checked the time and discovered he was up and about in the dewy dawn beyond common reason. He wondered why. He felt just fine, if a mite weak in the knees from bedroom athletics. The steak and potatoes he'd had before Dorothy were sitting right in his innards. He'd awakened early for some other reason.

He headed down the alley behind Dorothy's cottage toward the main street. He meant to check with Western Union, see if at least one of his borrowed ponies was up and about, and visit a few possible witnesses, unless his orders were to return at once to Denver.

When he'd worked his way back out to the main drag, he spied a small crowd ahead, down by the telegraph office near the railroad stop. He walked faster and when one of Sheriff Lansford's deputies spied him and called his name, he walked even faster. As he joined the crowd the deputy said, "We've a killing inside, Longarm." Longarm shoved through the crowd and entered the Western Union office.

Inside he found the sheriff and some others behind the counter, jawing with the telegraph clerk who'd been on duty the night before when Longarm had first arrived. They were staring down morosely at something on the floor. Longarm moved closer, peered over the counter, and saw another gent on the floor. He lay on his back, so there was no doubt about him being a customer of undertaker Dorothy. But the round that had taken him over the left eyebrow likely wouldn't call for much mortician's wax.

The sheriff nodded to Longarm and said, "It looks like a holdup gone sour. Western Union, here, says nothing's been took."

The clerk from the night before remembered Longarm and agreed. "I don't understand it," he said. "Old Charly's log says he didn't take no money in after he relieved me at midnight, for nobody sent no wires from here. Even more mysterious, he logged the few night letters as came in, and *they're* all here, too."

Longarm asked if any were for him. The clerk blinked. "Oh, sorry. I reckon this has me flustered, Deputy Long. Poor Charly did take down some messages aimed your way."

As he took the night letters from under the counter and handed them across to Longarm, the sheriff observed to nobody in particular, "Well, the single shot was heard by folks up the street just about sunrise. So the stickup gent or gents couldn't have rid far. We'd best saddle up and see if we can cut their trail on the infernally dry prairie!"

Longarm didn't answer as he read the two night letters. The one from Denver was as silly as expected. Billy Vail wanted him to find out what in hell had happened to the missing agency people and return to Denver at once. He didn't say which came first. The Indian agent at McLaughlin confirmed that agent Kruger, his wife, and Polly Bean's uncle were still missing, which was reasonable enough to say. But then he went on to ask Longarm to meet some extra Indian police in Middle Fork and show them the way to Standing Rock, which was just plain dumb.

In the first place, Longarm didn't work for the B.I.A. In the second, any Indian police officer who couldn't find a reservation as big as some states back East wasn't much of a tracker. He noted neither had Lakota names, either. The old B.I.A. was acting smart as ever. There was nothing like importing Indians from rival nations to question sullen Lakota who likely didn't speak their lingo.

Longarm tore up the two dumb night letters and asked the clerk who else might have gotten one before the dead man stopped taking messages. The surviving Western Union man consulted the log and said, "Big Mike Maldan got a wire from Dodge. One of his hands already picked it up. The only other one is from Washington, addressed to that Russian prince at the Triangle Crown. It's still in the basket."

Longarm knew Western Union had tedious rules about customers reading one another's messages. "I'll deliver it for you," he said. "I'm riding out that way directly."

The clerk handed it over. Longarm put it in a side pocket unopened for now as the sheriff asked wistfully, "Ain't you riding with me and my posse, old son?"

Longarm shook his head. "Nope. Two reasons. Mean-hearted as murder might be, it's a local offense, and you're the local law who gets the chore. My second reason is that I'm on a tight timetable and don't really have time to see all the folk I ought to about pure federal mysteries."

He didn't add that he doubted they'd cut any sign unless the killer was thoughtful enough to leave a paper trail. Assuming he'd even ridden out, and wasn't some local punk holed up here in town after a stickup gone wrong, the sun was already burning off the dew and the topsoil was hard as adobe brick right now.

He elbowed his way back outside, went up to the livery, and gave the colored boy on duty a dime to saddle up the painted Indian pony for him. He'd decided that while the buckskin was a better pacer, the paint was steadier. He didn't have too far to ride, and he meant to have solid horseflesh under him should anyone dispute his right of way.

He mounted up and rode, heeling the paint into a lope to pass Dorothy's funeral parlor sudden when he saw some of Lansford's deputies headed for her front door to tell her she had more business.

He reined to a walk beyond and saw the First Church of Salvation ahead, where she'd told him to look for it. The church was a bleak white frame building with a rectory as bleak attached to it. The burial ground was on the downwind side of the church. He saw a patch of bare earth by one marker, where the late Kiowa Kid likely reposed. A weary-looking old gent was digging a grave near the back fence. Longarm rode to the edge of the property to hail him. The gravedigger was more than willing to stand his spade in the dirt and come over for a chat.

Longarm said, "I hate to be the one who has to tell you this, but you've got two of them holes to dig today, pard."

"I heard," the gravedigger said. "I don't mind. I gets paid by the hole. What can I do for *you*, pilgrim? You don't look ready for my services just yet."

Longarm sighed, "Well, just give me some time. I was wondering if it's too early to call on the minister and his lady."

The gravedigger spat and said, "It is. They keeps banker's hours. Won't neither of 'em be up and about this early. In fairness, Reverend Parkman stays open late, should any souls need saving. You having trouble with your soul, pilgrim?"

Longarm shook his head. "I try to lead an upright life. I wanted to talk to them about the collection of Indian relics I understand they keep."

"Oh, that's Miz Mabel's hobby," the gravedigger said. "The minister ain't interested in heathen souls. But his wife's sort of artistic, or queer in the head, depending on how you regards collecting baskets, beadwork, and such. She won't sell you none of her Injun play-pretties, if that's what you're after."

"Ain't interested in buying Indian relics," Longarm said. "Interested in who's been selling 'em. You know a Lakota gal called Dancing Antelope?"

The old man spat again. "Yep. Not in the Biblical sense, but I must be the only unmarried white man in Middle Fork who hasn't had her at least once. I thought you said you lived upright, son. Can't you find something less disgusting to play with?"

Longarm laughed. "I'm not searching for her carnal, pard. I'm the law. Dancing Antelope is missing, along with some medicine objects the Strong Heart Society sets great store on. I was wondering if she'd brought 'em here to peddle. Would you be in a position to tell me?"

The gravedigger nodded and said, "I would, and she never. I don't just dig holes for a living, pilgrim. When things is more peaceable I acts as church sexton here. That means I gets to ring the bells and sweep the floors. So I can tell you Miz Mabel ain't added any junk to her collection of late, praise the Lord." He spat again. "That sassy breed gal ain't been by for some time now. You're sniffing at the wrong stump, pilgrim."

Longarm nodded, thanked him, and rode on, pondering his words. He'd noticed the missing gal's bawdy sisters looked a mite whiter than most Lakota. If folk in town considered the missing one a breed on sight, it meant she had to look even whiter. He told his mount, "It's starting to look more and more like she just put on a Dolly Varden dress and skipped the country, Paint. But we'll keep our eyes peeled for carrion crows just the same, right?"

The church lay on the edge of town, so they were out on the prairie as they followed the wagon trace said to lead to the Triangle Crown.

There were all sorts of hoofprints in the dust of the wagon trace. Any set of them could have been left by the rascal who gunned the Western Union clerk or, more likely, by innocent riders going every which way. That reminded him of the night letter the prince had received. He took it out, opened the flap carefully with a knife blade wetted with spit, and tried reading it.

He wasn't able to. The infernal night letter had been sent in pure Russian. Since Western Union had to use Roman letters instead of the funny Russian alphabet he was able to make out that the sender had been the Russian Embassy back East, but that didn't tell him much.

He resealed the wire and put it away again. At least it gave him a polite excuse to approach His Highness. Longarm had found in the past that most folk took some time opening up to a lawman if he just rode in empty-handed, asking questions, and the prince was said to be a proud, proddy rascal to begin with.

They'd said the rascal's spread was a good ways out to the north. So Longarm lit a smoke and settled down for some tedious riding at a mile-eating but discomforting trot. Trotting was easy on the mount, if rough on the crotch, and open prairie got mighty boring to stare at after a while. But knowing he might not be alone out here served to keep him awake with both eyes peeled. So when they'd traveled may-

97

haps eight miles and he spied big black birds circling to the west he reined the paint off the wagon trace to see what those carrion crows were up to.

They were circling above something down in a draw about a mile off the trail. He couldn't help hoping it was a dead cow. For Walking Willow and Cherry Basket were nice-looking little gals and he didn't cotton to the sight of their big sister staring at the sky with her eyes pecked out, even if it answered some important questions.

It was neither a dead cow nor a dead Indian gal he found when he topped the last rise and saw the crows were hovering because a coyote had claimed the kill down in the next draw. The coyote lit out as it saw Longarm riding in, so he didn't gun it. He knew the gent on the ground hadn't been brought down by coyotes. There was an arrow stuck in his chest as he lay on his back, trying to gaze up at the sky with no face worth mention.

Longarm dismounted, leaving the paint to graze at less than spooking distance as he approached the dead man. He whistled and told himself, *Old son, he sure ran into somebody that didn't like him, didn't he?*

The dead white man was dressed shabby, like a saddle tramp who'd sort of gathered what he could along the way from clotheslines and such. His shirt was too big and his pants were too tight. The boots he must have been wearing were missing. But his battered hat lay a few yards away as if someone had tried it on and skimmed it against the west wind, disgusted. The dead man had been scalped and then some. The killer had made the first cut at the base of the neck and just peeled off the scalp and most of the face, to the gaping mouth. The results sure looked horrid. For the crows hadn't gotten the eyes yet, and they stared up wildly from the red, raw skull. Longarm knelt for a better look at the arrow. It was fletched with owl feathers and striped with vermilion. He gingerly turned the dead man's hands palms up before he told him, "Pard, this don't make much sense. You was hit with a Lakota arrow. Then you was scalped Cheyenne, beyond the call of duty even for them. But a Cheyenne counting coup always cuts the bow fingers of a dead enemy, lest his spirit try to haunt 'em with Dream Arrows."

He tugged gently at the Lakota arrow. It didn't want to come out without breaking, so he let it be. There was no I.D. in the pockets. He got back to his feet, dusting off his tweed pants with his Stetson as he thought. Finally he told the dead man, "I ain't got time to ride all the way back to town and fetch the sheriff and undertaking gal for you, pard. But just be patient, and if nobody else has found you by the time I ride back this way, I'll pass the word."

He headed back up the slope to remount. The paint looked walleyed at him and danced off, dragging the reins sort of flirty. Longarm said, "Don't fun me, horse. If you're even considering running off to leave me afoot out here, it's only fair to warn you that you won't live to snicker about it, hear?"

The paint must have known he meant it as Longarm drew his .44. Or perhaps the calm words had a soothing effect. The paint steadied and let him back aboard her. So they rode on, cutting across country now.

They hadn't gone far when they topped a rise and saw a gully-whopper windmill on the horizon ahead. He heeled her into a lope and rode for the Triangle Crown. It had to be the Triangle Crown. Who else in these parts could afford a windmill mounted atop an oil derrick?

As they got closer, Longarm saw what the men in town had meant about the prince having a sod castle. He swung a mite to the west as he lined up on the imposing two-story building with a three-story tower erected at each corner.

The roofing was sheet copper not yet weathered green. It shone in the morning sunlight like burnished gold. Longarm smiled crookedly and thought, *For a gent who don't pay his bills, he sure lives pretty, don't he?*

Someone stationed in one of the watch towers must have spotted Longarm about the same time. For as he headed up the last rise his side of the layout, he saw a long line of riders had beaten him to the crest. They reined in as if to wait for him, so he kept riding. They were all wearing tall, fuzzy hats and long gray military topcoats, despite what the sun was commencing to do to the morning breezes, and, sure enough, they had cartridge loops sewn to their chests, the way Miss Pretty Blankets had said. He hadn't thought an Indian lady could have made that up.

As he approached, one of the cossacks drew a cavalry saber, waved it over his head, and shouted out, *"Nyet, nyet, vospreshchayetsya!"*

Longarm didn't know how to answer in Russian, so he just waved and called, "Howdy, gents," as he rode up to them.

They swung in around him from all sides as he reined in to face the one with the drawn saber. He noticed the others were drawing their own swords. He said, "Now, let's not get testy, gents. I got a night letter to deliver to your boss, see?"

He saw they didn't follow his drift when the leader snapped an order and they crowded him from all sides, stone-faced as Indians at a serious powwow. "Now look here," he said. But then a sneak swung at him from behind and, as the flat of a saber rang against the back of Longarm's skull, he suddenly found himself in the dark, wondering wistfully where he was and how he'd gotten there.

• • •

Like most men who'd learned to face death for a living, Longarm had learned not to dwell on just what might or might not be waiting for him in the great beyond. He'd often suspected, in a tight spot, that there was nothing at all in the big darkness, but consoled himself with the thought that if a man didn't know he was dead, it likely wouldn't bother him all that much.

So he was pleasantly surprised when he opened his eyes, still dazed, to find himself looking up at an angel gal. She was blonde and beautiful and, while she wore neither wings nor a halo, he doubted mortal hands had ever sewn that lacy white silk garment she was wearing. He was also surprised to note that angels were allowed to show more chest than one might see in church of a Sabbath. He figured the pearl choker about her long pretty throat was meant to make up for the fact that her tits were nearly showing above the lace of her white bodice. His head still rang like a bell and his lips were dry. But he licked them gamely and said, "Howdy, Miss Angel. I'm sure glad to see you and Saint Pete saw I meant well, despite my weak nature."

The angel spoke with a sort of French accent as she asked him how he felt and called him a poor thing.

He said he had to study some on that as he propped himself up on one elbow to get his bearings. "I think I was killed by cossacks. Danged if I know why, ma'am."

Then, as his eyes focused on his surroundings, he frowned and said, "Nope. That wasn't what happened after all. For I'm hurting too bad to be dead, and I see this looks more like a gal's fancy boudoir than any heaven I ever heard about, no offense."

"You are a guest in the palace of Prince André Deltorsky, Deputy Long," she said. "I am Natasha Petrova, his . . . friend. You may call me Tasha, since I wish to be your friend, too, *non?*"

He lay back to steady his weak-feeling stomach as he said, "I see you went through my pockets, since you know my name, ma'am. Did the prince get the night letter I brought?"

She nodded as he suddenly remembered he used to pack guns, felt for his derringer and side arm, and saw he'd been relieved of them as well.

"We are sorry our servants mistook your intentions, *m'sieu*," she said. "When you feel better, His Highness will receive you himself, to make amends, *non?*"

Longarm swallowed the green taste in his mouth, sat up, and ignored the impulse to vomit as he told her, "Let's get cracking, then. I have something to say to him, too."

"Are you sure you have recovered, *m'sieu?*"

"Nope. But if we wait till this lump on the back of my head goes down, His Highness and me will likely both be too old and gray to care what the other might have to say."

He lurched to his feet. Tasha steadied him. "You are either very stubborn or very strong, *m'sieu*," she said. "You took a *très* nasty bump on the head indeed."

"I didn't take it," he said. "It was given to me. But it would have felt worse if that cossack cuss had hit me with the edge instead of the flat, I reckon."

She led him out. He saw they faced a cavernous stairwell, shook his head to clear it more, and added, "No, it wouldn't have. Had he cut this fool head clean off it wouldn't be throbbing so. Is his infernal whatever downstairs?"

"Oui, he is receiving in the drawing room, *m'sieu."*

As they descended the stairs he asked her why she talked so odd, explaining, "I met some Russian immigrants a spell back, growing red winter wheat, and they had what I took to be regular Russian accents. No offense, ma'am, but for a Russian gal, you sure sound as French as a Red River breed."

She dimpled prettily. "Only peasants speak Russian in Russia, *m'sieu*. We of the nobility prefer to converse in French, like civilized people. Didn't you know that?"

"I do now, ma'am. It must cheer your common folk back home to know the folks ruling them think they talk barbarous. How do you tell one of your underlings to chop cotton or fetch you a fresh julep, ma'am?"

"Oh, naturally we know how to speak Russian, if we must. But you are right about it being a *très* barbarous language, *m'sieu*."

He didn't comment further, since he hardly ever expected to wind up riding for the Czar. For a place with outside walls of sod, the innards were fixed up fancier than pictures he'd seen of the White House back East. Longarm was no building contractor, but he could see it must have cost a pretty penny to panel all the walls with red and gilt like that.

The main floor was hardwood parquetry slick as a skating rink under layers of hard rubbed wax. To keep folk from slipping on it, oriental rugs were scattered across it. Tasha led him through red velvet hangings into a drawing room big enough to serve as a railroad waiting room. The walls were paneled the same red and gilt, save for floor-to-ceiling French doors along the east wall, affording a spacious view of nothing but dry grass as far as one wanted to gaze.

There was no throne. So the sissy-looking dude with all the medals on his Prince Albert coat was holding court by leaning one elbow atop the mantel of the baronial marble fireplace as he drank with the other. In case nobody could see at a glance how important he might be to the world, a big complicated coat of arms was carved in the marble above and behind him.

The other folk in the room looked more human. There were two men and four gals seated here and there on the

103

comfortable-looking furniture, all looking uncomfortable.

Tasha led Longarm up to the prince, who didn't offer to shake and didn't say he was sorry, but smiled and told Longarm to consider himself a guest. Longarm said he wasn't a guest, he was the law, and he had a few questions to ask.

Prince Deltorsky never blinked as he replied, sort of purry, "I have diplomatic immunity, *m'sieu*. I do not discuss my affairs with American authorities."

Longarm said, "So I've heard, Prince. Don't worry; I'm not here to collect for the many folk you seem to owe for services rendered. As you know from looking through my duds while I lay dreaming about your boisterous cossacks, I'm a federal deputy. I'm looking for some missing folk, and—"

"You bore me," Prince Deltorsky cut in. "Sit down and make yourself comfortable, but quietly, if you please. It is not my custom to pay my accounts more than once a year, or to discuss trade with my guests. Luncheon will be served shortly."

Longarm stayed put, even though the blonde gal was tugging at his elbow. "I didn't come out here to eat your grub, Prince," he said. "I come to ask if you and yourn have seen an Indian lady, recent. And, while I'm on the subject, I'd like to question your cossacks about the way another of them treated a Lakota gal who ain't missing, but happens to be mad as hell, anyways."

The Russian shook his head. "Out of the question. My men speak little or no English, even if I were to allow you to bother them, which I won't. As I said, I have diplomatic immunity. Me and my people do not have to answer to you for anything, *m'sieu!*"

Longarm met his steady, steel-eyed gaze long enough to decide the arrogant Russian was as stupidly stubborn as he sounded, and said, "Well, if you won't talk sensible, I'll just have to wire Washington and let them figure out how to deal with you, Prince. I thank you for the invite to lunch, but I ain't hungry. So if you'll just hand over my guns and tell me where my pony is, I'll be on my way."

Prince Deltorsky said, "You haven't been dismissed yet. *I* shall decide when anyone here leaves, if ever."

Longarm frowned, "Hold on, Prince. I don't know beans about this diplomatic immunity business, but it can't give you the right to hold me prisoner without a declaration of war, damn it!"

"Natasha, seat our guest somewhere and instruct him on his manners, lest I lose my saintly temper," the prince said.

The Russian gal tugged so hard she threw Longarm off balance as she pleaded, "Please, *m'sieu*, don't make him angry!"

Longarm was starting to feel hot under his own collar by now, but she, at least, was acting polite, so he let her haul him away and sit down with him near the two nearest gals.

He nodded to them, noting they both looked pale and scared as well as young and pretty. They both wore those bloomer-girl outfits meant for hiking across country in more civilized parts. Tasha murmured, "The prince is *très* upset about something in that telegram you delivered, *m'sieu*. He says no one is to leave until he digests it further."

Longarm asked quietly, "Are these other folk unwilling visitors, too?"

Both the bloomer girls nodded, ashen-lipped.

Tasha said, "You were unconscious for some time, *m'sieu*. These young ladies and the other two couples were brought in by our cossacks while you were recovering."

One of the bloomer girls leaned closer to whisper. "We hadn't done anything. We were just hiking our way to California when those awful soldiers charged across the prairie

105

at us. Oh, Lord, what's going on here?"

"I'm still working on it, miss," Longarm said. "Were you two young ladies crossing the prairie on *foot*, for God's sake?"

Her companion nodded and spoke defensively. "We had our packs, of course. Those soldiers took them away from us. How are we ever to get to California now?"

He shook his head in marvel. "They may well have done you gals a favor at that. Didn't your mothers ever tell you this is sort of wild country as well as mighty open?"

"We heard the Sioux have been quiet this summer."

"I'm working on that, too, miss. Leaving out what could happen to you in these parts, don't you know there's a mighty spacious desert west of the South Pass?"

He could tell they hadn't heard much about the Great Basin, so he turned back to Tasha to ask her what had been in the wire from the Russian Embassy in Washington. She said she didn't know. Prince Deltorsky didn't approve of other folk reading his mail.

Longarm shot a hard-eyed glance across the room at the prissy son of a bitch against the mantel. "I'm disapproving of him more by the minute," he said. "You look like a sensible gal, Miss Tasha. Can't you see your boyfriend's crazy?"

She shrugged her shapely bare shoulders. "What can one do, *m'sieu?* He is a prince of the royal blood. He is used to having his own way."

"Honey, that was in Russia. This is Dakota Territory. And even if you're willing to put up with his foolishness, he's holding seven U. S. citizens prisoner, whether he ever serves us lunch or not!"

"Oh, I am sure he will treat you all kindly as long as you don't annoy him. Resign yourself, *M'sieu* Custis. There is nothing you can do until His Highness gives you permission."

He decided she was crazy, too. He asked the nearest bloomer girl if the other two American men, seated too far away for him to jaw with, had been stripped of their guns, too, and if she had any notion where all the hardware might be.

She murmured, "Those two couples were picked up separately. The ones nearest are a rancher and his wife, stopped on their way to some town to the south. The couple by the windows say they live on a homestead near here. Both men did have guns when the cossacks arrested them. I don't know what's become of them since."

Longarm saw that the prince had a fresh glass of the lemonade or whatever he was drinking, and was drinking it pretty good. So he rose to mosey over and ask the other two men if they were ready to help him clean the sassy Russian's plow, barehanded.

Right then all hell busted loose.

Someone shouted and pointed out the French windows at a cossack riding toward them lickety-split. The prince looked just as surprised as it became obvious the gent on the leathered chestnut had no intention of reining in on the far side of the glass. The prince shouted, *"Nyet!"* The cossack, paying him no mind, rode right through the glass at a full gallop, jumped his mount across the table in the center of the room, and crashed, horse and all, against the far wall.

Horse and rider went down together as the gals in the room all screamed. The horse screamed, too, as it struggled to its feet, dazed, lathered, and cut by glass, to run wildly back outside, taking out another French door on the way.

The rider lay facedown against the wall he'd run smack into in his obvious desire to be someplace far from where he'd been when he took that owl-fletched arrow in the back of his long gray coat.

Other cossacks appeared in the shattered entry as Longarm strode toward the fallen man, crunching glass shards under his army boots. He knelt to feel the side of the cossack's neck as the prince and the others gathered around.

Longarm looked up and said, "Dead. Don't ever ride into a solid wall with an arrow head nestled close to your heart."

Prince Deltorsky shouted, "This is an outrage! I have diplomatic immunity, damn it!"

Longarm smiled crookedly. "With the Lakota Nation?" he asked.

"Lakota Nation? Are you talking about Sioux, you idiot?"

"Look, old Prince, you can call 'em anything you like. But one of 'em seems to have killed this poor cuss. He saved his hair, at least, by riding like the wind for home before they could count coup on him. Now would you please tell your other cossacks to stop gawking and man the goddamned defenses? This old boy was riding like somebody was *chasing* him, and no Indian by any name knows beans about diplomatic immunity!"

The prince just hopped from one foot to the other, like a little kid trying not to piss his pants. Natasha Petrova had sense enough to rattle out a string of Russian orders. The cossacks came unstuck and moved to the open, glassless side of the room, whipping out sabers, horse pistols, and such. Tasha had been asking questions as well as issuing commands. So when things got more sensible, she told Longarm, "Poor Sergei, there, was riding out to the east along with his comrade, Ilya. As you see, he came back alone."

Longarm nodded. "So much for Ilya's boots and scalp, then."

Prince Deltorsky stopped dancing to demand, "How could they have allowed such a thing to happen? They were trained cavalrymen!"

Longarm shrugged. "A trained cavalryman named George Armstrong Custer must have wondered about that not far from here, back in Seventy-six. Few Indians have had much cavalry training, Prince. They play by different rules. I'd say the one as done the deed on your two boys were likely laying doggo, disguised as a soap weed or a clump of nothing-much when he let 'em ride by, then let 'em have it from behind with a brace of silent arrows. They usually pick off the rider to the rear first. Then they arrow the other before he even notices a sudden lull in the conversation."

One of the cute little bloomer girls asked, "Oh, are they liable to attack us here?"

Longarm started to say no, but that would have been dumb. He stared out past the men guarding the smashed opening and made his voice sound more worried than he really felt as he said soberly, "Custer had a whole troop of cavalry with him at Little Bighorn. How many riders do you have, Prince? And, while we're discussing tactical matters, has anyone thought to man the other four sides of this layout?"

Tasha said other cossacks were on the walls above them.

"I have a troop, too," the prince said. "I brought thirty cossacks from my estate when I came over here."

Longarm said, "That ain't no troop. It's only a platoon. You'd best hand back the guns you took from me and these other gents, Prince. Us Americans know more than you about fighting Indians."

The other two male "guests" looked more sick than enthusiastic, but they were smart old boys and backed his play by at least saying nothing.

Their arrogant "host" shook his head. "Don't be ridiculous. Do you take me for a fool?" he snapped.

Longarm didn't think he ought to say what he thought the rascal was, with his armed retainers all about. So he just said, "Well, if you get us all killed, I'll never speak to you again."

Prince Deltorsky brushed imaginary flies from in front

of his face and snapped something in Russian at Tasha that sounded dirty. She took Longarm by the arm again. "Come, all of you. His Highness wants you all out of the way, upstairs. As you see, he is *très* upset. This is no time to argue with him!"

Longarm shrugged and let her escort him and the others out as the prince recovered at least part of his wits and commenced shouting orders in Russian that likely would have made any Indians listening nervous, too. Out in the hall, one of the other men asked Longarm, "Reckon we could make a break for it, pard?"

Longarm shook his head. "Don't jump the gun. Aside from Russian rifles trained on our backs as we left, we have to consider at least one mighty surly brave out there, and we don't have a slingshot to face him with between us!"

Chapter 9

The blonde Russian gal had left Longarm to his own devices in an upstairs guest room. The door wasn't locked and a servant gal called Matryona had even brought him a silver tray of tea and some prissy little sandwiches. But he was starting to get the distinct impression Prince Deltorsky liked to play iron fist in a velvet glove. So when he heard someone bawling in the next room, Longarm cracked the door and made certain none of those *dvorniki* gents, as they called the house servants, was in the hallway before he slipped out to learn what all the fuss was about.

He listened through the door paneling. One of the little bloomer girls was telling the other soothingly, "Don't cry, Felicity. I thought we agreed before setting out on this grand adventure that we were willing to face danger gallantly as any man, the way Victoria Woodhull says modern women should."

"I was ready to face rape, but nobody said anything about getting *scalped*, damn it!" Felicity wailed.

Her companion giggled. "Pooh, who'd want to scalp us, even if the Indians win? They'd be more likely to want to make love to us."

"Of course. You know I've always admired muscular

men, Petunia. But what if they shoot us full of arrows, like that poor man downstairs?"

"Why should they? We agreed it was safer in the long run not to carry any weapons but our heavenly bodies. Indian men can't be that much different from other men we've met in our travels. I'm sure they'd rather kiss a pretty girl than scalp her."

That made sense to Longarm. He knocked on the door. The braver one, who turned out to be Miss Petunia, let him in, saying, "Oh, it's you. Tell this silly girl that we're not all going to be scalped by Indians."

"That's likely true, Miss Felicity," Longarm said. "They tend to treat male captives a mite disgusting, but Indians have natural feelings towards women and children. Lakota do, at least. Ain't no Apache about, so why worry about 'em?"

The two girls got on either side of him and led him over to the four-poster. "I doubt we'll get ourselves captured by Lakota in any case," he went on. "It seems the prince saw us first, and between you gals and me, it don't seem likely they'd attack so many rifles forted up so good. The Lakota in particular learned not to do that at the Wagon Box Fight."

They seemed to find his words cheering. For the next thing he knew he was reclining on the bedstead between them, with both trying to kiss him at once.

The bold Petunia was brunette and sort of chubby. Felicity had light brown hair and a slimmer build under the loose bloomer outfit they both wore. He kissed them both back, to be polite, but said, "Ladies, I don't know what the three of us are doing on this bed at the moment. I admire you both. But right now we're prisoners in a house under siege by Indians!"

Sassy Petunia kissed him again and started groping for his fly while Felicity told him, "We're devotees of Victoria

Woodhull, and she says a woman has as much right as any man to live free and take life as it comes!"

He shoved the brunette's hand away from his fool pecker, hoping she hadn't felt it taking notice of her, and protested weakly, "Damn it, ladies, I know who Victoria Woodhull is. I've even read some of her writings on the subject of women voting, free love, and other astounding notions. But don't either of you have no sense of proportion? I'm as free-living a man as any, but there's a time and place for everything, and this ain't it!"

It was Felicity's turn to kiss him as Petunia said, "You men are all alike, damn it. You whistle and mock at every pretty girl as she passes the pool hall, but when you get the chance, you're as shy as any prissy schoolmarm!"

She had his fly open and was playing with his full erection now, so he couldn't lie. "I'm as willing a man as any, but no fooling, this is just plain crazy! What if someone should come?" he protested.

Felicity got up and scampered over to lock the door on the inside. "Why should they?" she said. "They told us all to stay up here out of their way, didn't they?"

Petunia wasn't saying anything. She'd gone down on him, and as she slid her rosebud lips up and down his shaft he knew he was a goner. So he sighed and started unbuttoning as Felicity turned, took in the picture with a giggle, and proceeded to peel out of her hiking togs. He saw she had light brown hair all over as she approached the bed, bold as brass. "Get out of the way, Petunia," she demanded. "I was first out of my bloomers, damn it!"

Her friend obliged her by rolling away to start undressing, too, as slender Felicity got atop Longarm, impaled herself on his now raging erection, and started sliding up and down it, crooning, "Oh, lovely. He's hung like a horse!"

Petunia laughed. "What did you think I just spit out, a

melon seed? Hurry up and come, dear. I'm hot and gushing, too!"

Longarm laughed wildly and, now that he was undressed and willing, rolled little Felicity over to do her right while Petunia played with his bouncing balls and kissed him all over his bare behind.

Felicity moaned as her companion flopped beside them and whimpered, "Now me! Now me, damn it!" So he just had to roll over once and finish coming in the softer, chunkier brunette. She clamped down on his shaft. "Oh, I felt that and I liked it, but for God's sake, don't stop now!"

So he didn't. It was easy enough to stay inspired in such good company. It was hard to say which had the nicest offering between her thighs, but the change of view did wonders for him. The sunlight was streaming through the window across the room, so no details were left to the imagination.

He and Petunia came together and, that making it twice in a row for him, he'd have been willing to slow down for now. But Felicity had gotten to running her fingers through her brown thatch, shamelessly, and as he relaxed aboard the brunette, she rolled over on her hands and knees, wagging her sassy rump at him to demand he do right by her some more.

He wanted to look out the window, anyway. So he got to his feet, took the fundamental matter of Felicity in hand, and started throwing it to her dog style as he gazed out the window across miles of what seemed to be empty prairie and, hopefully, figured to stay that way at least until dark. As he humped Felicity he asked, conversationally, if either knew what time it was. He'd been knocked out for some time and come to missing the watch chained to his derringer. But neither gal answered. They were too busy coming. So Longarm joined them.

114

Before anyone could start anything wilder, Longarm said, "Now let's all stop for a council of war, ladies. This is fun, but it ain't going to get us out of this fix, damn it."

Felicity started sucking him to see what it was like. "I wish men didn't talk so much in bed," Petunia said. "They told us to stay up here and behave ourselves, didn't they?"

He laughed, closing his eyes in pleasure. "We sure have been behaving some. But who knows what time it is, and where my infernal guns might be?"

Felicity couldn't answer with her mouth full, so Petunia said, "I think it must be about four in the afternoon. I don't know where your *other* guns might be. Felicity, don't waste that in your mouth, damn it."

But she did. For as the soft shapely brunette rubbed against him, purring and kissing, he exploded in the other gal's throat and thought he would surely pass out again.

But he didn't. Felicity choked and rolled away, gasping and spitting as the brunette entrapped him in her lush love box before it could droop.

Longarm gave up trying to talk sense to either of the bawdy bloomer girls. He said, "Well, seeing as we ain't been caught and don't seem likely to be, and now that we've got the foreplay out of the way, what do you ladies say to some serious screwing?"

Petunia gasped as he rolled her on her back, hooked an elbow under either knee, and opened her wide as she'd go to pound her hard, hitting bottom with every stroke.

Felicity sat up and said, "Oh, yum yum yum!" as the one he was in protested, *"You* take him like this if you want to, damn it! I don't care what Victoria Woodhull says. There are limits and...Oh, Jesus!"

So, after he'd treated the thinner Felicity the same way, finding she opened even wider, thanks to her longer thighs giving him more leverage, both gals said they'd had enough.

So he left them dazed and saddle-sore across the bed after he got dressed again to see what else the upstairs of Prince Deltorsky's house had to offer.

It didn't have much. He had no trouble looking in on the other captives. The nesting couple and the ranching couple had each been given decent enough rooms. The nesters had a different view from their window. The worried farmer said he'd spied some cossacks riding off to the south and asked Longarm what that might mean. Longarm said, "Two things. They were likely sent to scout and maybe bring back the body of that cossack killed over the horizon. It also means there ain't as many of the rascals here now as there were. How many did you see leaving?"

"I'd say two dozen. Why?"

"His High Unwholesome says he has about thirty. That means half a dozen cossacks and the servants here now. The odds are improving. But not that much, seeing they have guns and we don't."

"Have you considered making a break for it after dark, Longarm?"

"I surely have, provided I can figure how to get our guns and horses back. Leading two gents and four women to safety by the light of the moon, afoot and unarmed, don't sound safe to me."

"What if just you, me, or that other gent lit out alone to go for help, Longarm? The windows ain't barred, as you can see, and the sod below is soft enough to drop to."

Longarm shook his head and said, "We go together or we stay and study a better way, pard. You may have noticed our host is sort of proddy. So there's no telling what he'd do to the ones left behind if one of us upset him. I wouldn't bet much money on the one who just lit out afoot, neither. Both them cossacks and likely one or more surly Indians would be after him—mounted, armed, and dangerous. You folks just do as you're told for now. You got no choice."

The rancher had even less to offer and when Longarm moseyed to the stairwell one of the prince's *dvorniki* gents in livery was standing there with a gun and a wooden expression. So Longarm howdied him and turned to go back to his own room. He was feeling sort of tuckered anyway, for some reason.

He flopped on the bed and thought for a while. Then, since his thoughts were only chasing their own fool tails in circles, he gave up and had a nap. When he woke up again the Matryona gal was shaking him and it was dark out.

She didn't speak English and was sort of old and plain, so he didn't kiss her. He saw she wanted him to come with her, so he went. She led him downstairs to where he found the blonde Tasha and the other captives seated at a dinner table. The prince's imposing chair stood empty at the head of the table. Longarm sat down across from Tasha, who would have been seated at the prince's right, if the moody cuss had been there.

The blonde tinkled a bitty silver bell by her place setting and the hired help commenced serving everybody. The first course was soup made of beets that looked like Lakota war paint and tasted tolerable. The main course tasted even better, whatever in hell it was. Longarm nodded grudgingly across at Tasha and said "Well, I see His High and Mighty don't mean to starve us to death, Miss Tasha. What happened to him? Don't he eat with common folk?"

"He's ridden out to fight Indians," Tasha said. "He's recovered from his earlier shock, he says, now that he understands the situation. Our men found another white man dead out there on the prairie while they were looking for poor Ilya."

Longarm nodded and said, "I suspicion I met the same

117

gent on the way out here, if he was dressed like a saddle tramp. Since we're at table, I won't describe him further. If that's who your cossacks found, they rode a lot closer to town than we are right now. Are they all riding in a bunch, or what?"

Tasha shook her head. "Prince André has ordered patrols in every direction. I believe he led his own detachment out to the north."

Longarm washed down some of the beef he'd been chewing with some of the tea Russians seemed to serve in glasses instead of cups. "I figured he might, seeing as the nearest considerable concentration of Lakota lies to the south," he remarked.

The rancher had gotten over some of his first shock, too. He snorted in disgust. "I had a dog named Prince, once. Had to git rid of him. He bullied cats and run from other dogs."

Longarm smiled, but said, "Mind your company manners, pard." Then he turned back to Tasha and asked, "Did they ever find old Ilya, or is he still missing, ma'am?"

The blonde shrugged her bare shoulders and replied, "I don't know. His Highness doesn't consult me on every detail. None of them said they had, but I'm sure by now they must have. There's a full moon tonight, and how far could a dead or dying man have gone?"

Little Felicity, down at the far end, bleated, "Heavens, do we have to talk about dead people at dinner?"

So Longarm nodded and asked the blonde across from him, "What happens after dessert, Miss Tasha? Do we shoot pool, play charades, or didn't the prince say?"

She smiled wanly, and replied, "As a matter of fact he left no orders regarding you, except that the household staff and I should see that you remain here until he returns, of course."

"Oh, of course," Longarm said, adding, "I sure hope you and our other guards share diplomatic immunity with your boss, too, Miss Tasha. For, though it pains me to inform you so, there's a law in this country as considers holding people against their will a serious breach of the peace, called kidnapping."

The blonde shrugged again. "It's my understanding diplomatic immunity extends to everyone employed by His Highness, *m'sieu*. In any case, none of you have been kidnapped, you know. Everyone here was trespassing on Prince André's land when he or she was invited in to await Prince André's pleasure, *non?*"

Longarm said, *"Non*. Speaking for myself, I rode in on U. S. government business, which wouldn't be trespassing in any sensible court of law. As to these other folk, they may or may not have been inside the boundary claims of the Triangle Crown when they was captured at gunpoint by your riders. But that don't matter. Said boundary line is neither fenced nor posted. So, aside from local custom and common sense, statute law is on their side. No landowner can make a trespassing charge stick unless he's posted his property with signs saying he don't want you on said land."

The nester to Longarm's right said, "Me and my woman was on the wagon trace to Middle Fork, riding peaceable in our buckboard, when them crazy cossacks jumped us!"

"That's what I just said, pard," Longarm said. "Let's not all talk at once. I'm trying to make Miss Tasha, here, see how crazy her prince is. The rest of us are all agreed on that point."

So the farmer went back to eating as Longarm told Tasha, "You don't look crazy, ma'am, so you must be able to see that by this late date me and these other folk must have friends or relations wondering where on earth we're all at. With suspicions of Indian trouble in the air, some danged

119

somebody is bound to send out searchers, and what do you aim to do when *they* show up? I know it's a tolerable big house, but there can't be *that* many guest rooms."

Tasha looked uncertain, so Longarm pressed on. "I've never met your Czar Alexander, personal, but ain't he the gent as freed the serfs in Russia a few years ago?"

She nodded and said, "The Little Father is a saint, *m'sieu*. But what has that to do with us at the moment?"

"Just wondering how old Alexander is going to take it when he hears your prince is holding half of Dakota prisoner in this here robber baron's castle, ma'am. By the way, did you just say diplomatic immunity extends to the *hired help* of His High and Strange?"

She nodded, as he'd expected her to, so he asked innocently, "Where does that leave you, ma'am? I still ain't too clear as to your exact position on his staff."

Down at the end of the table Felicity giggled and Petunia murmured, "I doubt if he has a staff that's worth it. He drinks too much to be much in the feathers."

Tasha's face got as red as the beet soup they'd had earlier. She dropped her napkin beside her plate and rose grandly to march out of the room, stiff-backed, but sort of sobbing.

The rancher laughed. "Hot damn, that was telling her, little lady! I'll bet she's nothing but the prince's play-pretty!"

His wife snapped, "Sam, eat your dessert," as she got red-faced, too.

Longarm sighed. "Dang it, Miss Petunia, I was working on her pretty good when you insulted her away from the table!"

Petunia shot him a roguish look and asked, "How come? Aren't you satisfied with present company yet?"

He felt his own neck redden some as he replied. "I wasn't flirting with her. I was trying to spook her. The fool prince is out baying at the moon right now, and I was hoping she

120

and the others here might not be so crazy." He rose to his feet and put his hat back on. "I'd best see if I can find her and tell her how sorry you are, Miss Petunia," he said.

He headed for the doorway Tasha had left by. The *dvornik* standing by it looked uncertain, but didn't try to stop him. The nice thing about well-trained servants was that they didn't think for themselves, and nobody had told the Russian the rules on that particular doorway.

Longarm found himself in a long, dimly lit hallway he hadn't seen before. He headed down it, saw a door ajar, and opened it. The blonde wasn't inside. The room seemed to be a sort of office. A big, fancy desk was covered with ledgers and papers, all inscribed with those funny Russian letters, so Longarm didn't even try to read them. He helped himself to some cigars from a humidor of malachite, put them away just in case, and started to leave. Then he reconsidered, looked under the desk, and, sure enough, there was a wastebasket and the telegram he'd brought out was in it, crumpled in an angry ball. He put that in his pocket, too.

It was lawful, since the prince had thrown it away, and there was just no telling when Longarm would meet someone sensible who might be able to read it for him. He'd noticed it had put the prince off his feed for some reason.

He went back out into the hall. Ladies who leaped up from table mad tended mostly to flop down somewhere to bawl. He doubted there were any bedrooms on the ground floor. But the hall didn't seem to be leading him to any stairs. So where would she have gone? A fretful horseback ride in the moonlight didn't seem likely, with Indian trouble on the evening breeze.

He was running out of hallway when he heard sad singing ahead. He frowned and followed the sound to a door. It was Tasha, he was sure, singing something soft and lonesome on the other side. He opened the door. There was a flight of steps going down into darkness. Could the fool Russian gal be crooning like a lost gypsy in a dark wine cellar?

There was only one way to find out. He took out a waterproof match, thumbed a light, and eased down the steps as, ahead, Tasha went on moaning and groaning, louder now. She was either in desperate pain or starting to cheer up again.

He came to another door of heavy oak. Light showed under it. He shook out the match and knocked on it. On the far side, Tasha stopped wailing and called out in Russian. She sounded mighty angry. He tried the latch and opened the door to call out, "It's only me, ma'am. I'd like a word with you in private."

Then he blanched as he faced what seemed to be a solid wall of white smoke filling the room beyond. It looked like the fool Russian gal had decided to cremate herself alive!

He waded into the swirling mist, not breathing lest he choke on it. He couldn't see a thing. Tasha was wailing fit to bust, now, as well she might, so he groped his way to her, grabbed her, and discovered he was clutching a mighty damp and naked gal by one arm and a tit.

He realized his error, inhaled some air with a lot of steam, and let go of her. "Sorry, ma'am. I thought I was rescuing you from a fire. I see now that we're in a Turkish bath. Or is it a Russian bath?"

She answered by swearing at him in Russian and French. He knew enough French to understand the part about him being a pig, but he failed to see why she called him a camel as well.

He said, "Oh, simmer down, Tasha. I can't see a damn thing and I'll be leaving directly. But as long as we're alone—"

"You touched me!" she cried in English. "What do you mean by caressing my naked breast, you beast?"

"I ain't caressing it now, ma'am," he said. "I only want a word or two in private with you. I know you have to be careful in front of them *dvornik* fellows, but now you could be in big trouble."

She snapped, "For God's sake, shut the door then! The steam is escaping and I am getting a chill from the draft!"

He nodded, groped his way through the steam back to the door, and shut it. Then he turned around. She'd been right on the money about the air in here clearing some. For he could see her mistily now as she sat on a bench against the far wall. She knew he could see her and she had her legs crossed and her breasts covered with her hands. He looked away and observed, "This sure is a swell layout. Wood walls and all. I see the steam comes from them pipes along the baseboard. They'll have me blind again in a few seconds. So, like I was saying, Miss Tasha, you could be in a pickle when the U. S. Cavalry or somebody like it shows up to demand an accounting on us missing folk."

She protested, "Prince André has diplomatic immunity."

"Let's not talk tedious, Miss Tasha," he said. "What Miss Petunia implied at table was mighty rude and I told her after you left she should be ashamed of her fool self. But facts are facts, and if in fact you're nothing to either the U. S. or Russian governments but a fellow guest, I don't see how in thunder I'll ever be able to get you off."

She covered her face with her hands, forgetting he could still see what she'd let go of, and proceeded to bawl like a baby. So he sat down beside her on the damp bench, wetting his butt through his pants as he soothed her. "Please don't cry or sing no more, Miss Tasha. I can see the pickle you're in and I want to be your pal."

She leaned against him, getting him even wetter, as she

sobbed. "I am not a bad girl. I am property of Deltorsky family. I am nothing, only peasant."

He'd suspected as much even before her French accent had begun to slip. So he patted her warm, steamy naked back reassuringly and told her, "You may be what you say back in the old country, Miss Tasha. But in this country we don't keep human beings as property since the War. So let me ask you something, and I want you to think before you answer. If I could get you out of here, too, would you like to come along?"

"Where could I go?" she protested, not seeming to notice or care as Longarm's hand slid down her slippery back to rest more comfortably on her lush, round rump.

"Honey, a gal as pretty as you could write her own ticket in this land of opportunity," he said. "You talk good English when you ain't upset. If you ain't up to working for a living you could likely get all sorts of rich American gents to marry up with you."

She snuggled closer, her wet blonde head buried against Longarm's chest as she wet his shirt through his vest and all, and sobbed, "Who would marry me now? I was engaged to nice boy back in village. But Prince André wanted me instead, and what Prince André wants he takes."

"I've noticed that. Just for the record, has he mistreated you in other ways? I keep a mental list of woman beaters, just in case I ever meet up with them where the law don't have to know about it."

She shrugged. "He is treating me as decoration, not woman. He is not much man. He drinks too much, like that girl say, little pig. He dresses me like grand duchess and lets me order servants like mistress of *dacha*. But, oh, Custis, I am so not happy!"

He grimaced and said, "I ain't happy, neither. Aside from being held prisoner I'm getting wet as a drowned cat.

Could we get you dressed and out of here now, ma'am?"

"Is bad for health to leave steam bath too soon," she said. "My pores are just starting to open, and—"

"My pores are feeling just awful under this damp cloth," he cut in. "If you won't put something on, I'd best take something off. Where do you hang your duds around here, Miss Tasha?"

"Outside door, on hooks," she said. "Steam pipes in wall dry them while you take steam in here. But do you think we should take steam bath together, Custis?"

"I don't see why not. Matter of fact, I can't see *nothing* improper now."

He rose as she giggled and said, "All right, but no tricks. We just take steam together like good friends, *da?*"

He didn't answer. He never broke his word if he could help it. He groped to the door, stepped out, and felt in the dark to discover sure enough that Tasha's duds were hanging against steam pipes he hadn't noticed coming in. He shucked his own duds, shivering in the cooler dark of the cellar, even though he got out of the damp duds pronto.

He ducked quickly back inside. It felt a lot better now that he was naked, too. Opening the door had cleared the air a mite again, so he saw she was now in the corner with her naked back against the wall and her bare feet up on the bench. She must have been able to see him as well. She gasped and said, "Oh, you're so big."

She likely meant he seemed taller, slimmed down in just his birthday suit. He moved over to the bench and sat near her feet. "Say, this feels mighty fine," he remarked. "I try to keep reasonably clean, but to tell the truth I ain't had a real hot soak since I left Denver."

"You let steam open all pores, then you scrape skin clean, wait, and see how much more dirt comes out," she told him.

"I've taken a steam bath before, ma'am, albeit seldom with such pleasant company. I don't see you no more. Can you see me?"

She moved her bare toes against his naked thigh. *"Nyet,* but *there* you are. Tell me more about land of opportunity, Custis."

So he did, crossing his fingers when he said she'd doubtless be a big American star should she ever want to go on the stage back East. It was stretching the odds a mite, but it was at least possible, for she was mighty pretty and, he thought, intelligent.

She must have admired the pictures he painted for her with only a few little old white fibs, for as he described some of the delights of Denver she cut in thoughtfully, "I have no money, and if I run away from master and they catch me . . ."

He grabbed her bare ankle and shook it to shush her as he pointed out that the jewels she wore just to get about the house would keep most plain old American gals for a month of Sundays. "As for running away from masters, Prince Deltorsky ain't nobody's master in this land of the free, even though he can't seem to get the idea. I'll tell you what, Miss Tasha. If you'll help us get out of here, I'll buy you a ticket to Denver with my own money and wire ahead to have a brace of U. S. deputies meet you at the Union Depot there. I'm sure my office will take you under protective custody as a material witness, and once old Billy Vail has himself a material witness, he ain't about to give the same up to the Seventh Cavalry!"

She toyed absently at his steam-slicked hide with her naked toes as she said she didn't understand what he was talking about. So he explained. "You won't be under arrest—locked up or anything, Miss Tasha. The boys will just see that nobody bothers you, in case they ever want to ask you something, see?"

"I will be ward of government, like Indian?"

"Something like that. Only, being a white lady, you'll have more freedom. Naturally, once you get used to the notion of living here as a freed slave, my office will dismiss you as a federal witness and you can go anywhere and do anything you like. See?"

"I see. But is too good to be true! You are not telling Tasha all this to make big fool of her? You promise?"

He raised her bare foot and kissed her instep like it was her hand as he said, "The only one trying to make a fool of you is your infernal crazy Russian prince, Miss Tasha. You don't even need my help to skip out on the rascal. But I said I'd make it easier for you if I could, and I meant it."

He lowered her foot in his lap and continued to fondle it as he added, "Of course, to do anything at all, I have to get out of here first."

She wiggled her heel deeper in his lap as she giggled softly and asked, "Out of steam or out of *dacha*, Custis?"

He knew she could feel what she was feeling with her naked foot, so he rubbed it harder against his hardness as he chuckled and said, "I reckon we may as well finish this old steam bath right, first."

But as he slid his bare rump along the slick wet bench toward her she raised her bare knees between them and gasped. "Wait, what do you think you are doing?"

He said, "I thought I knew. But if I'm wrong, we'd best get the hell out of here, honey. As you just observed with your teasing foot, this steam has a mighty warming effect on a man!"

"You mean you want to make love to Tasha?"

He decided she wasn't likely to make it all the way to star on the wicked stage, after all, if she was *that* dumb. But he kept his voice polite as he replied. "I wasn't figuring on kissing nobody *else* in here, Miss Tasha. Look, I enjoy long engagements as much as the next man, but we don't have *time* for more than a quick one, if that. I ain't twisting your arm, damn it. I said if you was ready to get dressed, unfriendly, it was okay with me."

"Please don't be angry!" she pleaded. "Please don't leave Tasha here, now that you promise delights of Denver! I will do anything, anything, to be free woman!"

She must have meant it. The next thing Longarm knew she was on her knees between his own, doing scandalous things to his steamy erection with her lush lips and darting tongue.

He gasped and said, "Hold on, honey. Waste not, want not!"

He hauled her up on the bench, got into position, and entered her right as their slippery bodies slid together in mutual delight but a perilous position.

The bench under Tasha's steamy rump was slick as a slab of fatback and as she started moving it wildly from side to side as well as up and down, he saw they were likely to fall off on the hard floor. So he moved higher up her voluptuous, slippery torso, braced one foot on the floor well out to the side, and drew the other knee up between her rump and the wall above the bench. It gave him a mighty interesting angle of attack.

Tasha must have found it interesting as well. She moaned, raised her own limbs higher, and locked her ankles around the nape of Longarm's neck to raise her buttocks entirely clear of the hard wood as she matched his thrusts with passionate corkscrew gyrations of her own while she attempted to swallow his tongue and chew off his moustache at the same time.

He knew now that she'd been telling the truth when she implied the prince hadn't been at her lately. It was just as well. A woman screwing half so fine would have doubtless raised the dead, but thanks to his earlier and considerable adventures that day he was content to let her do most of the real work as he just moved his hips at a comfortable lope. A man who'd started from scratch in anything that sweet, hot, and active would have come in ten good plunges or less. She seemed grateful to observe he was lasting longer than most. Like most women, she took it as a compliment. As they came up for air — or steam — between kisses, Tasha crooned in Russian, then switched to English to say, "Oh, Custis, Tasha so happy to see you not jackass rabbit, like other men, phooey!"

He kissed her some more to shut her up as they went on not being jackass rabbits. He wondered what other men she'd had after the prince had taken her from her intended back home. He didn't ask. It just meant he didn't have to worry, later, about a semi-innocent immigrant gal in the big city. He could see, too, why other men might have failed to satisfy her. For a gal so active-hipped, and so obviously hard up, she took a mite longer than most gals to get there.

But at last she did, and when she did, the surprise drove her even wilder. She bucked so hard the next thing he knew he was flat on his back on the floor with Tasha squatting over him, bare feet flat on the wood to either side of his hips as she played stoop tag on his organ grinder to literally jerk him off with her whole bouncing, steamy, sweat-slicked, naked body, until he came so hard his head started hurting again.

She rolled off, laughing, groped for a bucket under the bench, and stood over him with a bare foot planted on either side of his chest as she raised the bucket high, poured it over her own head, and gave him a shower as well when the water — cold, damn it — ran down her naked curves to spatter him from face to groin.

He gasped, "You might have warned me!" as he felt goosebumps rising all over his cleaned-off hide. But the

129

steam and Tasha warmed him again in no time when she turned to face his toes, dropped down atop him with her fundamentals staring him full in the face, winking, and proceeded to swallow his shaft alive again.

He let her. He was too beat to move, and if she enjoyed trying to blow tunes on a flat flute, he considered himself a good sport. He had to keep her on his side, if she was, so he started playing with her insides as she spread her steamy thighs wider for his inspection and attentions. She seemed to find it satisfactory when he massaged her bitty pink clit with two fingers of one hand as he slid first two, then three, then four fingers of the other in and out of her. She stopped what she was doing long enough to moan, "All of me! Outrage Tasha's everything!"

So, as she commenced to inspire his other probing tool with her lips again, he decided she could only mean that one way. He hooked the thumb of the active hand into the only other opening available and, from the way she moaned and wiggled her rump, that had been what she meant, sure enough. She seemed to be a mighty wild gal, and the view was downright shocking. But, what the hell, since she was steam-cleaned all over, it was good, clean fun, he decided.

Her own outrageous behavior down at the other end of his body had worked it up again for him, impossible as that had seemed. So in the end they wound up finishing right, with her head and shoulders on the bench as she knelt on her knees, spine arched, to take it like a love-starved gal.

She would have taken more had not Longarm insisted, "We got more serious riding to do before morning, Tasha. Tell me first where the bastards have our guns as we get cleaned up and out of here, hear?"

She splashed more water over them both and handed Longarm a towel as she explained why he'd never see his or any other gun the prince had locked up in the cossacks' armory. "Is guard on duty. Cossack, *nyet dvornik*. I can show you unguarded door leading out to stables. We go now, *da?*"

He wiped himself tolerably dry. "Not just yet," he told her. "I don't mean to leave the others to the mercy of a maniac, and I paid good money for my guns and watch."

"Custis," she insisted, "you can't have guns and watch. You crazy to even think of others at a time like this."

He led her out and as they dressed in the dark he said, "You've been hanging out with crazy folk so long it's only natural that you don't know crazy from right, honey. You can't ride off dressed like an infernal princess. Do you have a riding outfit? Good. You'd best put it on and, while you're at it, stuff all the jewels into it as you can carry comfortable. But first show me where that gun room is."

"On far side of stable," she said. "Is too complicated running back and forth like chickens with no heads, *nyet?*"

"You're right. First we go upstairs, get you and the others fit to ride, and *then* I'll see about our goddamned guns."

Chapter 10

Getting the guns back was easy. Once Longarm had Tasha and his fellow captives set to depart, the Russian girl showed them how to sneak down the back stairs and into the dark stable. Then Longarm had Tasha call to the guard from the dark and, recognizing the voice of the mistress of the house, the fool naturally stuck his head out of the armory to see what she wanted. Longarm hit him just hard enough to knock him out without insulting his diplomatic immunity permanently. The other two men suggested finishing him off or at least tying him up, but Longarm said, "He'll be found right soon in any case, if they stand guard mount as sensible as most soldiers. Let's get our infernal guns and get out of here before they get around to relieving him. Most guards in most units stand two hours on and four hours off."

So they did, helping themselves to some extra ammunition while they were about it. Then they just slid open the stable doors quietly and lit out on the same transportation they'd arrived with, save for Tasha, who was riding side-saddle on a chestnut thoroughbred the prince was likely to miss more than her. Tasha had put her French accent back on along with her handsome black velvet riding habit, so

Longarm knew she was calming down some.

The two bloomer girls had arrived on foot, so they got to ride in the buckboard with the nester and his wife. The other couple had been captured riding cow ponies and left the same way. Longarm had considered swapping the Indian paint for a fancy thoroughbred, but decided the paint knew him and his McClellan best. This was no time to break in a new mount.

They rode clear of the sod castle without incident, heading south by moonlight over the silvery sea of grass. Tasha had just remarked that it all seemed too good to be true when Longarm, who'd learned the hard way to look behind himself once in a while, said, "It is. Some rascal just topped a rise back yonder waving his pretty, shiny saber at the moon."

The nester whipped the rump of his draft horse with the reins, but Longarm called out, "Simmer down, old son. There's no way on earth you'll outrun gents on thoroughbred with that buckboard. So let 'em guess where you are for a minute or two. Don't signal your position with a clatter of useless racket."

The rancher drew his .45. "If you and me was to make a stand, here, Longarm, we might hold 'em off until the others got away," he suggested.

Longarm didn't think it polite to call a brave man a fool, so he just said, "I got a better idea. You lead everybody down into the next draw and keep 'em all still a few minutes. I'll see if I can play the old prairie hen with a busted wing trick on 'em."

The gals didn't understand, but the other two men had birded on the High Plains in their time, so they didn't argue. They just moved on, and when the nester's wife wailed something about them all being about to be hacked to bits by swords, her husband told her to just hush.

133

Longarm sat the paint where he was until he saw it was already sort of hard to see his fellow escapees. Then he rode east along the rise until he was well clear of them before he drew his .44, fired it at the moon, and called out, *"Kikikikikiyaha!* I'm a bloodthristy Crooked Lance and I'm out for cossack hair!"

The cossacks who'd been trailing the buckboard's sign across the moonlit grass didn't act scared at all. He could see now that there was a patrol of a dozen when they all raised their glinty swords in the moonlight and charged at him in a bunch.

That had been the general idea. A buckboard didn't have a chance of outrunning them. An Indian pony had perhaps forty—sixty odds, with the odds in their favor. So Longarm lashed his mount across her butt with the rein ends and said, "Come on, Paint, move your ass!"

There was a lot to be said for riding either an Indian or cow pony versus a thoroughbred. His smaller, tougher mount could turn inside a smaller circle and, for a short distance, dash faster. But the reason horse races were raced with thoroughbreds was that the big, dumb brutes *were* racehorses. He knew he couldn't outrun the men who were now chasing him with considerable enthusiasm. So it was time to play hide and seek. He rode to the top of a rise, reared the pony in the moonlight, and fired off another round, yelling awful things about their poor old Russian mothers, before he headed down the far side at an angle, reversed his course by whirling the Indian pony the other way, and streaked along the bottom of the draw the way he hoped they wouldn't think he was headed.

They didn't. When next he came up for a look the cossacks were riding to cut him off, had he been dumb enough to ride that way. He dropped down behind the swell with a chuckle and rode the paint east at a restful trot. She was likely wondering why he was acting so crazy, so he told her. "The game's not over yet, Paint. We still want to draw them away from the others, see?"

He rode her to the top of another rise and stood in the stirrups to see the cossacks going over another one, well to his north. So he stayed on the skyline, rode on in line with them until he saw more sabers waving in the moonlight, then cut back down, heeled the paint into a lope, and got ahead of them as they popped back up about the same time.

He didn't want them coming south. The others were headed that way. The game had drifted far enough east by now for some real diversionary stunts. So he waited until they dropped out of sight again before he loped the paint due north across their wake. He meant to circle them to the north and see if he could get them to chase him back toward the sod castle for a change.

It didn't work out quite as he planned. As he rode up a slope to show himself again, he met a cossack coming down it at him at full cavalry charge, waving a saber and shouting like a Comanche.

Longarm swerved his mount with his knees as the man on the bigger horse bore down on him. So it helped a mite that he was almost out of range when the cossack swung his considerable blade. Longarm did most of the serious avoiding himself, swinging himself out of the saddle on the far side as the saber cut through the space his head and shoulders had just occupied.

The paint, being Indian, was used to that kind of sneaky riding, and so he had no trouble guiding her as he cut across the wake of the cossack's thoroughbred. The Russian was a good rider on a good mount, so though his momentum had carried him on down the slope some, he reined in and spun his bigger mount, scowling at the sight of what seemed in the moonlight to be a pony without a rider. He rode back up to have a word about it with Paint, meanwhile staring about puzzled at the otherwise uninhabited prairie. Longarm held the paint still, broad-side to the oncoming throughbred. Then he danced her backward around to the cossack's left and swordless side before he swung back up into the saddle and whacked the cossack good across the nape of the neck with his own pistol barrel.

The cossack lay on the grass restfully once he hit the ground.

Longarm grabbed the reins of his thoroughbred. "Come on, horse," he said. "That was mighty slick of you two to fall out of the column and lay for flankers. Let's see if we can work out some *more* fun and games."

He topped another rise farther west, and sure enough they were all lined up to the east, having a powwow about where in thunder he might be now. Longarm moved down the slope toward them so they wouldn't see much against the skyline. Then he struck a match and lit one of the big, fat cigars he'd helped himself to in the prince's study. Someone shouted as he spotted the flare. Longarm had hoped he might. He puffed the cigar to get it going good, then stuck the unlit end under the rear skirts of the cossack saddle before letting go the reins.

The thoroughbred whinnied in discomfort and did what any horse with its ass on fire might have been expected to do. It bolted for home.

Longarm steadied his own mount and stayed put in the shadow of the rise. He watched the wind-whipped cigar end receding in the distance like a railroad tail light. He said, "Easy, girl. They can't see us, I hope. I know that was a mean trick to play on an innocent horse. But he don't figure to suffer half as much as yours truly if they don't fall for it."

They did. Longarm grinned as he saw the cossacks riding

to head off the runaway illuminated horse. They weren't about to catch it this side of the stable, of course. It was running under an empty saddle and no doubt inspired some by that lit cigar. He wondered what those cossacks thought they were chasing. But they weren't chasing him or anybody else important any more.

He let them ride clear out of sight before he swung his paint about and rode for Middle Fork. He took his time, knowing his mount had been put through more than the usual calls to duty, and that the others were sure to beat him there in any case.

He hadn't had time to tell anyone where to meet him, if they all made it. He assumed Tasha would have sense enough to wait at the sheriff's office and that the bloomer girls would have figured out by now that getting to California on foot was a mite more trouble than it was worth. He wondered if the three gals had compared notes on him. The sassy bloomer girls would likely think it humorous. Old Tasha might be upset. But that was something that couldn't be helped, when you parted sudden from gals without time for explanations.

By the time he was halfway to town he'd decided he hoped all three of them would be sound asleep by the time he showed up. He told the paint, "Don't ever make love to three gals in the same evening if you mean to ride a McClellan saddle, Paint. My private parts will never be the same!"

They topped another tedious rise. He reined in with a frown as he spied other riders, lots of other riders, coming his way from the south. He knew it couldn't be the cossacks. He patted the paint's neck and said, "Steady as she goes, till we see if it's time to run some more or not."

A distant voice called out, "There's one of them Rooshin sons of bitches, now!"

Knowing he'd been spotted, and not by cossacks, Longarm called out, "I ain't a Russian. I'm the U. S. law. Who in hell are you?"

"That you, Longarm? Big Mike Maldan here! Me and the boys just learnt from your friends how them sons of bitches treated you all. So we come out to fix 'em."

As the night riders joined him, Longarm said, "Can't let you do that, Big Mike. I already fixed a couple more than diplomatic immunity provides for, and, as you see, we all got away safe and sound, so—"

"That ain't all the sons of bitches done!" Big Mike cut in. "You know that undertaking gal, Miss Dorothy?"

"What about her?"

"She's been kilt! The doc says she was raped as well! Witnesses seen a gent wearing one of them cossack outfits creeping in from the alley ahint her cottage earlier. Time they run and got the law, it was too late. Sheriff found Miss Dorothy dead enough to be her own customer, and the place had been ransacked as well!"

"Sheriff said he don't hold with night riding," one of the others said. "But it's a free country, Longarm. So are you fixing to try and stop us?"

Longarm felt to make sure his Winchester saddle gun was still with him as he swallowed the awful taste in his mouth. "Nope. I'm riding with you," he said quietly.

When they got to the sod castle the Russians there disappointed everybody by sending out the old gal called Matryona to see why the boys were shooting out all the windows like that. They couldn't shoot an old lady waving a white pillowcase on a broomstick. So they held their fire and the old gal turned out to be a sneak who could speak English after all.

She said the prince was out and that neither she nor any of the others left had done anything calling for such boisterous behavior. Longarm told her he could likely keep the night riders from burning the spread if the cossacks alone surrendered. She said there were only a dozen on the premises and they had diplomatic immunity.

Longarm sighed and said, "Ma'am, I want you to listen tight and not say anything silly until I'm done. These gents here are not paid-up peace officers. They don't know beans about the laws of your country or mine. But they *do* know that one of their own has just been murdered by a man in a cossack overcoat and, to tell you the truth, I don't care if the son of a bitch is related to your Czar personal! So I'll tell you what we're going to do, ma'am. You send out your cossacks with nothing but air in their high-held hands. Then I mean to arrest them and carry them in to town for a hearing. Any who turn out to be innocent have nothing to worry about. If we can hang the killing on one or more, one or more will hang for it if I have to provide the rope—and the hell with my badge!"

She started to say something. He snapped, "I said not till I finished, and I ain't finished, ma'am. You tell your people that if they'd rather make a fight of it, that's what I come for. You might add that once said fighting starts, I won't have much control over these gents with me. On the other hand, if they're willing to do things my way, I'm giving you my word that not an innocent cossack hair will get hurt."

He nodded curtly. "I'm finished. You ain't, until you open fire or surrender. So what's it gonna be?" he asked.

She said she'd give the gents in the house the message and turned to go back in, running.

Big Mike growled. "Hold on, Longarm. Who told you you was in charge of this night riding expedition. And why can't we have some fun with the sons of bitches, innocent or otherwise?"

Longarm's voice was friendly as a sidewinder's rattle as he said quietly, "Don't fuck with me, Maldan."

So Big Mike didn't, and in a little while the Russian cossacks left behind by the prince all surrendered.

Chapter 11

It was shaping up to be a long, hard night by the time they herded the cossacks to town and put them in the Middle Fork lockup. The witness who lived across the alley from the late Dorothy Dobbs couldn't say which one she'd seen opening poor Dorothy's back gate earlier. Longarm hadn't asked the old gal who spoke English to come to town because he'd figured Tasha would be in Middle Fork to jaw with them. But when he asked about her it turned out she'd hopped the first eastbound train without so much as a thank-you note for him. She likely meant to become a stage star in a hurry. Or, to be fair, maybe she'd just been spooked.

The nesting and ranching couples had gone to bed somewhere in town. Nobody knew what in thunder had happened to the bloomer girls. Longarm didn't worry about that. None of his fellow captives had spoken Russian, and they all had tolerable alibis for the murder of the undertaking gal.

Some of the Russians likely could prove they were innocent, too, if only they could talk sensible. Before going up to Dorothy's to search for sign, he went to the Western Union to see if any messages had come in for him while he'd been kidnapped.

Big Bear and another wearing the badge of the Indian

police were waiting for him there. Big Bear said, "We thought you'd either come here or to the saloon, and they won't serve Indians in the saloon. This is Pashungo. The B.I.A. sent him to help. I need help. The agent and his wife are still missing."

Longarm shook with the other Indian policeman and said, "Howdy, Pashungo. You Shoshone or Snake?"

"No, I'm Northern Ute. From the Ouray Reservation," Pashungo said.

Longarm tried not to show his disgust, not with the likely innocent Indian, but with the B.I.A. for sending another enemy of the Lakota to police Lakota. In the Shining Times the Utes hadn't just been enemies of the Lakota, like the Crow. The Lakota called Ute their *favorite enemies* and set more store by Ute hair than the scalp of a white man.

"What about that trader, Bean?" he asked Big Bear.

The Crow said, "Oh, he's still missing, too. He's not as important. His niece, Miss Polly, is nicer to people. But we *need* our *agent!*"

"Yeah, it is about that time of the month again, ain't it? I sure wish you gents had your own mystery figured out. For I've got a bad one up the street! I'll tell you what. Stick around and help me look for sign and as soon as I figure out which foreigner to hang I'll ride back to Standing Rock with you and we'll see what we shall see."

Big Bear nodded and they followed him inside. There was a short wire from Billy Vail telling Longarm to get his ass back to Denver directly, and a longer, more interesting one from the State Department in Washington. He wondered how they knew him by name as he read it. Then he grinned and told his Indian sidekicks, "I knew the message I delivered to that Russian son of a bitch did something to his digestion! I don't have to worry about reading it now. The Russian government has revoked his diplomatic immunity after getting so many complaints about the crazy way he's been acting. The State Department wants us to pick him up and deliver him for deportation. Ain't that a bitch?"

Pashungo said, "If he read as much earlier and ran away, he will probably be riding for the Chicago Pacific railroad stops on the far side of the Cannonball Divide, no?"

"Good thinking," Longarm said. He picked up a pencil and telegram blank to jot down a message for the lawmen in better position to head the rascal off. He handed it to the Western Union clerk. "No hurry. Send it night letter if you like. It's good for the economy for the son of a bitch to spend as much of his money as he can before he has to go back and explain his manners to the Czar."

Pashungo frowned and asked, "Don't you want us to ride after him, if he just murdered somebody, as you said?"

Longarm had already noticed that the otherwise nice-looking Ute had the hunting eyes of a coyote or an eager lawman. Pashungo was obviously a breed, with as much white blood or more than the Falling Star sisters. That reminded him of something else. "The prince never murdered nobody," he said. "He's just a natural pain in the ass with a vile disposition and a yellow streak. He won't get far. Forget him. I just thought about that missing Indian gal, Dancing Antelope. Them infernal Russians has distracted hell out of me of late. You gents hear anything more about her?"

Pashungo looked blank, so Longarm knew he hadn't heard about that case yet. The Crow, Big Bear, said, "We've decided she just ran off to live white. The trader, Bean, might have run off with her, for all we know or care. They were both pests. But the agent and his wife—"

Longarm cut him off. "Later. Let's solve one infernal case at a time, gents."

So the Indian policemen followed him up the main drag

to Dorothy's undertaking establishment. A brace of town deputies were on guard, of course. The sheriff had given up and gone home for the night.

Since Dorothy had owned the place, she occupied a place of honor on her erstwhile work table, under a sheet. The other bodies had been set aside, for now, on the floor. The deputy who'd gone in with them explained that the sheriff had wired an undertaker to come over from the next town up the line to restore some order come morning.

Longarm lifted the sheet from Dorothy's face. Someone had thoughtfully closed her dead eyes, but her face was still a mask of blotchy purple. She'd been choked to death. Her clothes were ripped half off. He didn't look further down. The doc would have had reason enough for saying she'd been raped.

The Indian police poked about unobtrusively as Longarm and the white deputy discussed the case in circles. The deputy couldn't tell Longarm anything he hadn't already heard. Pashungo suddenly dropped to one knee and picked something up from behind a sheeted body.

He said, "Hair. Blond hair. Let's see if any of these others have blond hair."

Longarm said flatly, "They don't. And Miss Dorothy, as you just saw, was a brunette. Can you tell if that hair you spotted with them sharp eyes come from a he or a she, Pashungo?"

The Ute held the almost invisible single hair up to the light. "No. The end is broken. It could be the hair of a woman broken short in some struggle, or just the shorter hair of a man to begin with."

The deputy said, "Hot damn. That lets all the black-and red-headed cossacks off, don't it, Longarm?"

Longarm shrugged. "Maybe. Could be a hair from a recent customer of Miss Dorothy, just as easy. All sorts of heads have passed this way in recent memory—some living, some not. They might know at the church if she buried any blond folk, recent."

Pashungo glanced down at the floor. "Not possible, unless it was today. Look at that floor, Longarm."

Longarm did and said soberly, "Yeah, Miss Dorothy was neat, as I remember. That floor's been mopped and waxed within the last twenty-four hours. Thanks, Pashungo. I have other questions to ask at the church in any case, but it can wait, for tonight."

Big Bear asked, "Are you going to talk to those Russians now?"

"How?" Longarm answered. "I don't speak their lingo and they don't speak mine. But, like I say, none of 'em figure to go anywhere, soon. I reckon once we've cracked this case we'll be able to turn the survivors over to their own government. Meanwhile they'll keep."

Big Bear pointed at a match stick on the floor with his toe and said, "Waterproof match, like cowhands or others who camp out a lot carry."

Longarm nodded. "Already noticed it. Don't mean much. This happens to be a cowtown, pard. It's getting late. The killer doesn't seem to have left much sign, and by now he could be most anywhere. Do you two gents have some place to sleep lined up?"

Big Bear said they'd planned to sleep over their ponies in the livery. Longarm knew Dorothy's perfectly serviceable bed was just out back, and figured to stay empty a spell. But it might not look right if he were to make himself so free with the estate of a lady who'd been killed.

That did remind him, however, that they hadn't looked through the dead gal's personal quarters. He mentioned it to the town deputy and was told the sheriff had tossed Dorothy's cottage for sign without finding much, save for

145

some sheets in the hamper that might indicate the dead gal had been entertaining male visitors of late.

Longarm agreed soberly that if the late Dorothy Dobbs had led a more active social life than folk in town had assumed, it was not a matter for the law to mess with.

He'd about decided the livery hayloft was his own best bet when the sheriff came busting in, excited. "I was hoping to find you here, Longarm," he said.

"I thought you'd knocked off for the evening," Longarm said.

The sheriff said, "So did I. A homesteader west of town just rode in, waving one of them owl-fletched Sioux arrows. I'm gatherinq a *posse comitatus,* and—"

"Back up," Longarm cut in. "Start at the beginning, not with the infernal solution, Sheriff."

The older lawman nodded sheepishly and explained. "Earlier this evening, while you was playing tag with cossacks and I was taking notes on that dead lady ahint you, the homesteader I just mentioned stepped outten his soddy to take a crap. As he done so, a Sioux arrow thunked into his doorjamb. So he shut said door in a hurry and crapped in his pants, inside, instead."

Longarm whistled softly. "A surprise like that could upset one, couldn't it? What happened next?"

"Nester tolt his woman and their two kids to lie under the bed whilst he doused the lamps and manned the one window by the door with his good old repeating rifle. He heard war whoops and by the light of the silvery moon seen a nekked Injun on a hoss circling the soddy like it was a wagon camp. The Sioux put another arrow through his bought-and-paid-for windowpane. So the nester fired back, and he thinks he hit the son of a bitch."

"What do you mean, *thinks?* Did he put him on the ground or no?"

"Well, you know how confusing it can get in a firefight,

Longarm. The poor sodbuster had shit in his pants and busted glass in his hair when he fired in tricky light. The Sioux swung off the fur side of his running mount, either winged or riding sneaky the way they tends to at such times. Anyway, the Sioux must have been discouraged by a hit or a near miss, for he rid off and never come back."

Longarm glanced at the two Indian policemen. Pashungo's hunting eyes were glittering like a coyote who'd just sighted a sick sheep.

Big Bear frowned and said, "I think we must be talking about one crazy Indian, even for a Sioux. Hear me, that was no way to attack a house at night, alone." He turned to the sheriff. "Did the homesteader have any livestock?"

The sheriff nodded. "He rode in on some of it, once he'd changed his pants and waited long enough to make sure the Sioux wasn't coming back. He rid to a neighboring homestead where they had two husky sons to spare. Then, once he had his family and property under guard, he rode into town, mad as hell."

"Hear me, let's go get that Sioux!" Pashungo said.

The sheriff said, "That was the general idea, chief. I'm gathering my posse now."

The Ute shook his head. "We don't need a full pack of hounds to chase one fox, Sheriff. There are four of us, six if you count your two deputies here. One frightened homesteader was enough to send him on his way, wounded or not. I think we should go after him now. I think we should try to cut his trail while it's still fresh!"

The sheriff looked at Longarm and raised a questioning eyebrow.

Longarm said, "Makes sense, even though reading sign by moonlight can be a chore. We know where he started from, this time, and how far could he ride in the few hours he's had, wounded or not?"

The sheriff nodded. "Let's go, then. Nester's right outside. So that makes seven if he's ready to go home now."

Longarm shook his head. "Five. Leave your deputies here. This crime site needs 'em more than we do. Pashungo's right about the odds being tolerable."

The Ute smiled, friendly as a sidewinder closing in on a pack rat. "Let's go, then. I am a good tracker, and the Sioux took my father's hair when I was little."

Chapter 12

Indians weren't given to false modesty, and more than one had bragged a mite to Longarm in the past about mustard he just couldn't cut, when push came to shove. But when they got out to the homestead and found everybody safe and sound, Pashungo just circled the spread once on his chestnut stud and called out, "This way! He rode southwest. Wounded."

Longarm told the nester to stay with his wife and kids now that he'd shown them this far, and let them confirm that the arrows imbedded in his property were not only Lakota but made by the same arrowsmith.

Longarm, the sheriff, and Big Bear joined the Ute under the light of the silvery moon. Pashungo pointed at the ground, which just looked like a mess of moonlit earth to Longarm. "Unshod pony track," he said. "Blood on that grass stem."

Longarm squinted. "On what grass stem?" he asked.

The Ute swung down, still holding himself aboard the stud with one knee, to pluck an invisible object from the ground. He straightened up again and held it out to Longarm, who took it from him. Sure enough, it was a stem of dry straw, sticky with something that looked black by moon-light.

Longarm handed it to the sheriff, who whistled. "By the Great Horned Spoon, chief, you're *good!*"

Pashungo said, "I know. He went that way. Do you want to catch him, or do you want to sit here telling me how much you admire me?"

Longarm said, "Take the point, Pashungo. We'll back your play."

So the Ute did. As he rode southwest out ofj earshot, Big Bear muttered, "Don't be upset by his manners. Some breeds don't know how to act with either their red or white brothers."

Longarm said he'd noticed, and followed Pashungo with the others trailing. As he rode, he kept his eyes on the ground ahead for sign. He didn't see much. The night was dry as well as dark, so not even the big stud ahead was leaving enough sign in its wake to matter. Now and again Longarm spied a clump of weed growing a mite flatter than usual. Considering this was cow-covered open range, that wouldn't have excited him enough to matter, if left to decide for himself. But the Ute sure rode like a man who knew where he was going.

Longarm turned in the saddle to ask Big Bear if *he* saw anything with his sharper Indian eyes.

The Crow shrugged. "Utes are like that. People who hunt Mormon crickets and jackrabbits in the Great Basin must be used to smaller tracks than people who grew up hunting real meat."

The rider out ahead reined in on a rise and waited for them. When they joined him, he pointed. "There. I told you he'd ridden off with that homesteader's bullet in him," he said.

Longarm squinted down into the shady depths of the draw

150

to the southwest and, with some effort, finally made out a dark blob that from up here could be most anything. "Cover me. I'll see if he's really down or laying doggo," he said.

But Pashungo snaped, "*I* found him. He's *mine!*"and spurred his stud down the slope, chanting, "Kikikikikiya-haaaaaa!"

So Longarm and the others followed at a walk as the tracker who'd found whatever he'd found dropped off his mount to kneel in the moonlight over the downed man.

As Longarm rode close enough to see what Pashungo was doing, he called out, "Damn it, Pashungo, you're supposed to be an Indian *lawman,* wearing pants as well as a badge!"

But Pashungo straightened up, holding the scalp in one hand and a wicked-looking bowie in the other as he called back. "Hear me, I count coup! His people took my father's hair. Now I have taken his!"

He certainly had. Longarm dismounted for a better look and saw the gent on the ground was an Indian, full-blooded, naked save for a breechclout and considerable vermilion paint. His hair was cut short enough to line up for his reservation rations without getting fussed at, save for the neat little divot Pashungo had carved out for some fool reason.

Longarm asked Big Bear if he recognized him. The Crow got down for a closer look, shook his head, and pulled off the dead man's breechclout to expose his genitals. Longarm started to ask if he had two crazy savages riding with him before he caught on and said, "Right. Good thinking. But I knew it couldn't be that missing Dancing Antelope as soon as I noticed there was no tits in evidence."

Big Bear straightened up. "It pays to make sure," he said. "Some women are flat-chested, and we knew the missing girl was crazy, too. I don't understand this at all, Longarm. First Dancing Antelope steals old medicine from the Strong Hearts. Then another crazy person starts shooting arrows that haven't been made for a long time at people. I had what I thought was a good idea, but now it won't work."

Longarm smiled at the Crow. "I see I'm not the only lawman who's learned to play with his cards close to his vest. I considered that, too. Few gals would have had the strength to drive arrows into the wood back there at the homestead so deep."

He looked about and added, "Speaking of which, there ought to be at least one archery set around here somewhere."

They fanned out in the moonlight, kicking at weeds. The sheriff was the one who found the bow and quiver, lashed together, in a clump of soapweed. He was so proud he nearly busted his shirt buttons as he waved the kit in the moonlight, calling, "Here she is. Only two arrows left. But they're the same make and model!"

Longarm had a look, nodded, and said, "Well, we done what we rode out to do. We can borrow that nester's buckboard to carry this cuss back to town. Ain't it awful how the bodies keep piling up, now that there's no undertaker working in Middle Fork?"

He remounted. As the others did so, Big Bear asked his fellow Indian policeman, "What are you going to do with that damned scalp? I don't understand why you took it in the first place. It was the white man back at that homestead who killed him."

Pashungo's voice was defensive as he answered. "I promised my mother I would take at least one Sioux scalp when I grew up. I know I can't take it to the Old Ones for a feather now. Old Ones who live on the blanket of the Great White Father don't give feathers any more. But a promise is a promise, and . . . To hell with it. You are right. I just got excited and wasn't thinking straight."

He threw the scalp away in the dark. Longarm didn't say anything. It wasn't exactly destroying evidence. The Indian back there had been dead long before the overheated Pashungo had lifted his hair, so what the hell.

Longarm didn't get to spend what little was left of that night with Indians and horses after all. On the way back to town with the dead Indian the sheriff invited him to bunk in the guest room at his own place. The sheriff's wife even served flapjacks and Canadian bacon for breakfast. So the two lawmen got an early start in the morning, feeling chipper. As they were enjoying coffee and smokes a deputy came to the kitchen door to report the undertaker from up the line had arrived and wanted to get in Miss Dorothy's before the sun warmed things up. So they went to see about it.

The new undertaker looked more like what an undertaker was supposed to. He said his name was Novak and when they shook his hands felt cold as any of his customers might have once embalmed. The sheriff let him in to review the results of the recent mortality statistics of Middle Fork and Novak rubbed his cold gray hands together and said he was ready to get cracking. Neither lawman wanted to watch a once pretty lady get drained, so they went back outside.

As they were pondering their next move, a rider came in from the west, waving a fuzzy cossack hat. They noted with interest that he had a long gray topcoat lashed to his saddle as well. As he reined in, the sheriff said, "Morning, Jeb. Where you find them Russian duds?"

Jeb dismounted. "Up the railroad tracks about a mile or more outside of town, Sheriff," he said. "There was a thoroughbred gelding grazing in the middle distance under an empty saddle. But when I tried to catch its reins it outrun me and Lucy, here."

The sheriff nodded and said, "Thoroughbreds is like that.

153

What do you make of it, Longarm?"

Longarm frowned thoughtfully. "All indications point to a gent dressed cossack boarding a westbound freight from aboard a fast mount, shucking his giveaway duds before or after grabbing a ladder on the run."

The sheriff agreed he read it the same way. Longarm saw Big Bear and Pashungo coming up the walk at them and waved before he turned on his heel and went inside to call out, "Hey, Mr. Novak, would Novak be a Russian name?"

The undertaker looked up from the awful things he was doing to poor old Dorothy. "No, I'm Polish. At least, my folks were. Why do you ask?"

"Two reasons. Does Polish sound anything like Russian, and do you talk it worth mention?"

The undertaker went on with his grim work. "I can find my way to the saloon in Polish, and my Daddy once said it was about as close to Russian as Spanish might be to Portugee. What difference does it make?"

Longarm handed him the telegram he'd taken from Prince Deltorsky's wastebasket and asked if he could make out the funny words. The undertaker studied it, moving his lips, and said, "It's a good thing it's in Roman letters, like my own kin used in the old country. I can't make out every word, but the drift is that the Russian Embassy in Washington wants some prince to get him and his princess back to Washington pronto, to answer serious charges about abusing some privileges and disgracing hell out of his class, whatever class he graduated from."

Longarm nodded, said that squared with a more sensible wire he'd gotten in plain English, then frowned. "Hold on. Are you sure that scolding mentions a *princess* as well as a *prince*, Novak?"

"Hell, the lingo's not *that* different," the undertaker said.

154

"Says right here he's to bring Princess Natasha along to answer for some jewels she ordered from a gent named Tiffany and never got around to paying for. But you say you already heard all about it, so what the hell."

Longarm sighed. "It's hell indeed, and I'm a fool. For I seem to have helped a no-good princess escape while she slickered me into giving another no-good time to do the same! I'll be back directly. Got to send me some wires. You hurry up here. I've got more work for you in other parts, Novak."

As he left the undertaker called after him to ask who he meant to gun next. Longarm didn't answer. Outside, the two Indian police had joined the sheriff. Longarm told them, "Got to send some wires. You gents can stay here or ride on back to the reservation, where I'll join you in the sweet bye and bye. There's not much for Indian police to do here now. But I got to tidy up before we scout for them missing reservation folk."

They said they were going that way, anyhow, so as the three of them headed for the Western Union by the depot, Longarm went on. "I know the Princess Tasha hopped an eastbound after slickering me with a made-up accent and a story I feel mortal ashamed for buying. With all due respect to the Chicago & Pacific, she's going to have to change trains to get anywheres important. Her lover boy will have caught the same line, albeit the northern branch on the far side of the Cannonball Divide. There's no way they could have caught the same train. So, let's see, the best place for them to meet up would be Aberdeen, where either could wait for the other in a decent hotel and leave with the same via any of the half-dozen lines out of that big junction."

As he stepped up on the Western Union porch, Pashungo said, "Wait. I have been thinking. They both would have made it to Aberdeen by now. Not even the Chicago Pacific runs that slow. They've had most of the night, so..."

Longarm said, "You're right. I ain't awake yet. We'd best set the net a mite wider. Chicago would be where they change trains heading for New York, which don't seem smart, but it's worth a stakeout. I'm betting on Frisco. Old Tasha seemed mighty interested in the Golden Gate when I suggested it, during a moment my defenses was down just shameful."

"What about Denver and the border beyond?" Big Bear asked.

Longarm entered the telegraph office and grabbed for pad and pencil. He shook his head. "She knows Denver's my home base, and I can't see 'em running for Mexico. They like to live grand, and Frisco's about as grand a place as a flashy blonde can live without standing out."

He wrote an all-points and handed it to the clerk, who read it aloud to make sure he had it right. Longarm said he did and turned to leave.

Big Bear frowned. "Why did you say to be on the lookout for a good-looking blonde with an accent and a dark, snooty unknown but wanted man with cold gray eyes, Longarm? Doesn't that prince have a name?"

"Not till we catch him," Longarm said. "It's so dumb sounding I'm pure ashamed of myself, but I'm sure the butler done it."

The two Indians exchanged puzzled glances. "I've been to many a fancy home in my time," Longarm said. "Shacked up with a New York society gal one time as well. But I was so mad at being treated so strange I just never stopped to wonder where the infernal butler was!"

Pashungo asked him what butler they were talking about, so Longarm explained. "I was raised sort of plain. But I just now recalled how folk raised more lavish don't think it proper to boss their hired help about in person. They hires

156

fancy butler gents to do it for 'em. Yet the only critter in pants giving orders to the household help out there was the snotty rascal introduced to us as the prince himself!"

Big Bear asked Longarm what he thought might have happened to the missing butler.

"The butler wasn't missing," Longarm said. "He was acting the part of the missing *prince!* The real Prince Deltorsky had likely been buried, stuffed, or whatever, after catching the princess and her butler boyfriend taking a steam bath together or something. Whatever happened must have happened sudden and unplanned for. They were sort of playing it by ear and running scared as they tried to finish cleaning out the estate before they had to explain just what went wrong with the marriage to the moody secret police of the Czar."

Pashungo laughed. "Then you showed up with that wire telling them their time was up! That must have really driven them out of their wits!"

Longarm shrugged and said, "It wasn't a long drive. Had the two of 'em shared the wits of an honest half-wit they might have lasted a lot longer. But they was too dumb, too greedy, or both, to act half-wit decent! They needlessly riled all sorts of folk who wouldn't have knowed the real Prince Deltorsky from any other foreigner by letting his bills pile up unpaid. They refused to control their rough cossack cowhands. Then, even before they tried to hold a federal officer prisoner, they'd took to rounding up innocent travelers who someone was bound to miss and come looking for sooner or later. So what wits are we talking about?"

Pashungo asked if Longarm had any idea why he and the others had been taken prisoner. Longarm nodded. "That's easy, albeit dumb as hell on their part. They'd sold off the herd and, feeling guilty, feared someone who'd been on the land might mention here in town how few cows were to be seen these days on a cow spread owing money from here to Russia. I don't know what in hell they figured on doing to us all in the end. But between the wire from the Russian Embassy and the extra Indian scare, they must have decided it was time to just light out in all the confusion."

Big Bear said, "I understood half of that. Do you think the other servants were on it with them, or just dumb?"

Longarm said he didn't know and that it was time to find out. So they parted friendly and he went back up the street to get Novak.

The undertaker said he was busy, but Longarm insisted the dead could wait on the living, and in the end Novak went with him. The sheriff out front went too, puzzled.

They of course went to the town lockup, ducked inside, and waited till all the cossacks in the cage stopped yelling. Then, with Novak sort of translating, Longarm started taking notes.

As he'd hoped, for the sake of the taxpayers and an already over-crowded prison system, the Russians had been slickered, too, by the treacherous Tasha and her butler boyfriend, whose real name turned out to be Lavrenti Kaganovich. Longarm made Novak spell it twice.

The cossacks and other servants had known all along he was the butler, of course. Not even foreigners were *that* dumb. But as one of the excited cossacks explained, they'd been trained to take orders from the princess and her butler, so they'd gone on doing so when old Tasha had told them her husband was away on business for the Little Father and they weren't to breathe a word of it to any infernal Americans.

Longarm had Novak ask if they'd suspected Tasha of taking steam baths with old Lavrenti. From the shocked way they acted, it had never crossed their minds. The house servants, if any were still out at the Triangle Crown this

158

late in the game, had likely known more about the sleeping habits of the mistress of the house, but, like most well-trained servants, hadn't been trained to question them.

Longarm asked Novak to find out if they'd ever found that missing cossack, Ilya, and if he'd had blond hair. The answer was no and yes. They'd never seen hide nor hair of old Ilya after his comrade rode in with an arrow in his back. But he did have blond hair, now that they studied on it.

Longarm turned to the sheriff and said, "You may as well let 'em go. The Russian Embassy in Washington will likely wire you what they want done with the poor ignorant cusses. But I don't see what *we* might want with 'em now."

The sheriff agreed. "I can build with blocks, too. Two cossacks was out riding when they was jumped by Sioux. They split up and done some riding hither and yon, trying to get clear. The one as took the arrow didn't. His blond pard did. But instead of riding back to the Triangle Crown he decided to desert. Can't be much fun to be a peon, even on a thoroughbred. So he gave up the cowboy life in favor of a new career in crime and, damn it, he started with some *pissers,* and by now he's way the hell off, dressed human!"

Longarm told him to add his description to the now known name of the treacherous butler, if he wanted to. Then he went back outside to get away from all the sobbing coming from the cage as Novak explained to the prisoners how they weren't likely to wind up in a salt mine after all.

The sheriff asked where he was headed now. Longarm said, "I'm about done here. Have to ride back to the reservation and tidy up that mess. Before I do, though, I'd best have a word with the minister's wife about her Indian relics. Still have to account to the B.I.A. for a missing Lakota gal, and I'm getting mighty tired of running back and forth."

They parted friendly, too, and Longarm walked on up

to the First Church of Salvation. A nice old lady with pale gray hair was watering her dying flowers in the rectory yard. Longarm was pleased to learn she was indeed Mabel Parkman and that she was pleased to meet him, too.

She invited him in, sat him down by a rosewood table, and poured him some tea as she showed him all the Indian goodies she'd bought from various Indians passing by in the past. Some of them should have been ashamed of themsleves. They'd sold her not only busted-up baskets but what looked to be goods robbed from scaffold graves as well. When he commented on it, the sweet-looking little old lady smiled ghoulishly and opened a cupboard to produce a human skull. "It's a shame to waste things of scientific interest on the prairie winds and rains, Deputy Long," she said. "This is the skull of a noted medicine man named Kongra Seela. Don't you admire his lovely bone structure? Classic High Plains cheekbones, and he must have had a very noble nose."

Longarm repressed a grimace as he agreed soberly, "That's an Indian skull, sure enough, ma'am. What I wanted to talk to you about was some national treasures missing from the shed of the Standing Rock Strong Hearts Society. Miss Dancing Antelope lit out with 'em. You'd tell me if she brought 'em to you, wouldn't you?"

The old woman nodded sweetly. "Of course. I'd just love to get my hands on real ceremonial objects of the Strong Hearts. Alas, they consider them such strong medicine they never even leave them on a scaffold grave."

"I know. In other words, Miss Dancing Antelope never made it this far with her stolen gear?"

"I haven't seen her recently. She did sell me a lovely Berdachee fan a few months ago. Let me show it to you," she said.

Longarm started to tell her not to bother. He wasn't

looking for any missing Berdachee, as the Lakota called what ruder white men called infernal queers. But she already had it out and was waving it at him. "Isn't it beautiful? Look at that delicate beadwork on the handle. Nobody seems to spend as much time trying to look grand and feminine as those poor, confused Berdachee boys. You know what a Berdachee is, of course?"

He nodded and said, "Yes, ma'am. For folks said to be savages, most Plains Indians show surprising delicacy about the feelings of sissy boys our kind shuts away in prison for, uh . . ."

"Sodomy," the old woman said, calmly pouring more tea. "As a minister's wife, I find that shocking, too. But as a self-taught anthropologist I must say the Berdachee Lodge is a fascinating solution to the problem of what to do with people who simply seem to have been born perverse."

Longarm didn't think he ought to be talking about such matters with a minister's wife, no matter how motherly she might be. He started to change the subject. Then he took a closer look at the fan she kept waving and asked, "How can you tell a Berdachee fan from just a plain old flirty Lakota gal's, Miss Mabel?"

She smiled, sort of dirty for a minister's wife, and said, "By the design of the beadwork, of course. Berdachee are allowed to act as women and dress like women, since the Lakota consider them Woman-Hearted Ones. It's even permitted that a . . . well . . . lonely young brave might use a Berdachee as a woman on occasion. But since most normal men don't care for such outlets, Lakota feel it's only fair a Berdachee warn prospective suitors that they're really flirting with a boy."

Longarm supressed a smile. "I follows your drift, ma'am. In other words, since most Lakota men can tell a Berdachee from the real thing by its beadwork, a Berdachee might feel

161

free to flirt with most anyone who didn't seem to mind?"

She laughed sort of lewdly, considering. "Exactly. The Indian culture is so rational, once you consider some details we don't have in our own. I'm afraid a white boy with the same problem has to just take his chances if he wants to make a new . . . friend."

Longarm nodded, gasped, then snapped his fingers. "Suffering snakes! That's it! I should have seen it right off!" He got to his feet. "I sure thank you, ma'am. For you've put a mighty important piece of the puzzle in place for me and I'm so mad at my fool self I could stomp my hat. But if you'll just excuse me, ma'am, I ain't got time."

She showed him out and he legged it back to the undertaking parlor a lot faster than he'd left it. Novak was working on the cadaver of the dead saddle tramp taken first to the sod castle by the cossacks and then back to town by Big Mike's boisterous crew. Longarm said, "I know that poor cuss ain't got a face. But can you tell me for certain it's a man you're working on?"

Novak frowned and moved the sheet further down the now nude body. "See for yourself. Did you think he was a *she*, for God's sake?"

"Just had to make sure," Longarm said. "It's starting to look like I've been the victim of a mighty complex shell game. That one gets buried in the pauper's corner of the churchyard, right?"

Novak nodded. "I'm embalming him anyway. Sometimes folk come forward to claim such mysterious dead and it's a real pain in the ass to exhume 'em overripe."

"I'm going to have to ask you to do that anyway," Longarm said. "Miss Dorothy told me she just dropped the late Kiowa Kid in the ground the way he was. I'm deputizing you to have him dug out for a more thoughtful examination."

Novak wrinkled his nose and said, "Gee, thanks a lot!

What the hell are you expecting us to find after all this time? I understand he was already falling apart when they planted him."

"I don't want to influence your professional opinion," Longarm said. "You just have a look, then wire me at the McIntosh Agency on Standing Rock Reservation. I'll fix it with Western Union before I ride and take along fresh battery acid to fix things at the other end as well."

He looked at his watch. "I'd best get cracking if I'm not to dwell the night on the lone prairie. I can't hang around any longer. But before you plant that one, I'd take it as a considerable favor if you took time to autopsy him for exact cause of death."

Novak blinked. "Longarm, I don't know how to tell you this, but I just took an arrow out of his back, with considerable effort."

"Have a peek at his innards anyway. I got to ride."

Chapter 13

He did, driving the paint and buckskin harder than any thoroughbred could have taken as he switched from one to the other every few miles. It was rough on Longarm's rump as well, but otherwise more tedious than eventful. He stopped to water the ponies and coffee himself at the homestead where the plain young widow and her even uglier granny still resided safe and sound. They said they hadn't seen any Indians, save for the two Indian policemen passing each way. Longarm figured Big Bear and Pashungo were only an hour or so ahead of him, by now. He thanked the ladies and rode after them. The sun was low in the west.

He almost caught them on the prairie. They'd been riding serious, but perhaps with more consideration for their ponies. They'd just dismounted in front of the McIntosh police station when Longarm rode in to do the same. As he tethered his jaded ponies he nodded to them and said, "Howdy. My ass is sure sore. Since yours must be, too, let's just walk over to the agent's. I got some battery acid in these bitty bottles. By now they must have finished some chores for us up to Middle Fork. So I'll fix the telegraph set and find out what they found out."

The three lawmen walked the short distance with the

sunset painting their long shadows purple on the ground before them. Big Bear said he didn't have the key. Longarm told him not to worry about it.

He picked the front door lock and led them in. The house smelled musty and worse. Pashungo sniffed. "There's something dead in this place, Longarm," he remarked.

Longarm said, "Yeah. When I was here before it wasn't so strong. I thought it was spoiled food."

The young Ute breed sniffed again and shook his head. "That's not spoiled food I smell. Nothing smells like a dead body but a dead body!"

Big Bear nodded and said, "*Heya*, my Ute brother is right. Where do you think that stink is coming from?"

Longarm said, "Cellar. Dirt floor. There's a coal shovel down there, too, if you gents would like to have a look. I'll be in the office, fooling with the telegraph."

They split up. Longarm helped himself to water from the kitchen pump and refilled the empty wet cells over the agent's telegraph set before dropping in the dry acid. Doing it the other way could result in a small but nasty explosion of acid steam.

He gave the wet cells time to start juicing, and when he tried the set he had a live line again. So he tapped out a signal to Middle Fork.

The Western Union clerk in town was sending a return message when Big Bear and Pashungo rejoined him, grimfaced. Longarm ignored them as he went on transcribing the dots and dashes into block letters on the missing agent's pad. When he finished he swung around in the swivel chair and asked, "All three, or just the agent and his wife?"

"Two men, one woman," Pashungo said, "badly rotted and bloated under two feet of soil. They must have been buried a long time to have spoiled so badly."

Big Bear frowned. "My Ute brother speaks the truth.

But I don't understand it. Nobody has been missing that long."

Longarm pointed at the refilled wet cells above and explained. "The killer tried to get out of serious digging by pouring battery acid over the remains. As we smelled, it was a dumb move. The sulphur in the acid just added to the stink after it ate all it could before losing its strength in the lime soil."

Big Bear wrinkled his nose. "It still left them smelling terrible. How did you know all three had been buried under the house, Meneaska-Washtay?"

Longarm sighed and said, "I didn't know, for certain. I was sort of hoping I was wrong and that things could have happened the way I'd been meant to suspicion. I'd been given to understand the trader was a sort of worthless rascal given to sudden unwholesome impulses. So there was an outside chance he'd murdered the agency folk and lit out, after a fuss about the way he'd been abusing his Lakota customers."

Longarm leaned back more comfortably. "I had a time buying the notion that a posse of full-grown sharp-eyed Indians couldn't cut the sign of any damned body aboard a white-shod mount heading any damned where from here. But he was an Indian trader, who may well have known some Indian tricks. So I had to keep an open mind until I knew for sure where in hell he was. Now that I do, you'd best go arrest her and lock her in your station, Big Bear. I got to wire the other agency to send white B.I.A. officers up to make it formal, no offense."

Big Bear frowned and demanded, "Meneaska-Washtay, who on earth are you talking about?"

Longarm swung around and switched the set back on as he growled, "Thunderation, Big Bear, ain't it obvious? Miss Polly Bean has to be the killer. Who else is left? She told me she was a poor innocent, stuck with all the chores at her cruel uncle's trading post. What she really was was a lady who wanted to own her own business!"

As Big Bear stood silently, adding it up in his head, Pashungo frowned and asked, "Why did she have to kill the agent and his wife as well as her uncle, Longarm?"

Longarm shrugged. "She'd know better than me. If Trader Bean wasn't really her uncle, the agency folk might have known too much for her to inherit without considerable explaining. Or the agent might have wanted to send 'em both packing. Lord knows he had reason enough. She told me her uncle set the outrageous prices. Maybe he did. Maybe the agent called 'em both to his office for an accounting and the business discussion got testy. When I last passed this way I noticed she was a sort of impulsive little gal. But, hell, why are you gents asking *me* why she done it? Once you arrest Miss Polly, you can ask *her!*"

Big Bear nodded grimly. "Let's go, Pashungo," he said. The two of them left.

Longarm wired the other agency about the pending arrest, then patched himself into the Western Union grid to wire his office in Denver that he'd about wrapped things up and would be on his way home directly. He'd just finished and swung around in the agent's swivel chair to face the doorway when Pashungo came in, grinning. "White women sure yell a lot when they're arrested," he said. "Big Bear has her in the cage. You were right about her not being the dead trader's real niece. She was his common-law woman and they hadn't been getting along to well of late. She feared he planned on getting rid of her. So she decided to get rid of him instead. The agent and his wife had to be killed along with the trader because you were right about them knowing she wasn't the lawful heir to the trading franchise here."

Longarm sighed and leaned back further in the swivel chair as he said, "I sure am disappointed in Miss Polly. Is Big Bear getting it all down on paper, lest she try to reword it for her future judge and jury?"

The breed in the doorway smiled thinly. "He is. He sent me back over to see if there was anything I could do for you here."

Longarm's voice remained conversational as he nodded and said, "There is. I want you to unbuckle your gun rig and let it fall to the floor. For you're under arrest for impersonating a peace officer, and other crimes too numerous to mention."

The man in the doorway did no such thing. Having the advantage over a seated man with a cross-draw .44 wedged snugly between a hip and chair arm, or thinking he had, the breed slapped leather, his face a twisted mask of surprised rage.

He looked even more surprised when Longarm shot him twice at point-blank range before he could draw.

He slid slowly down the doorjamb to his knees with his shirt front smouldering as he stared in dying horror at the little brass derringer in Longarm's big right fist. The derringer was smoking, too. The tall deputy rose to his full height and said, "That's right. I had this out of my vest and palmed in my hot little hand all the time. I was hoping you'd prefer not to come quiet. For Miss Dorothy Dobbs was a pal of mine, you son of a bitch!"

The man on his knees tried to say something, but all that came out was a wet, froggy croak as his lips formed the word "Mother." It wasn't clear if he was calling for his own mother or insulting Longarm's mother. It hardly mattered once the dying man flopped limply on his left side in the doorway and finished dying.

As Longarm reloaded the derringer he heard running

footsteps coming their way. He'd just snapped the little gun back on the chain it usually shared with his watch and put it away in his vest when Big Bear came in. The Crow blinked in surprise at the dead man oozing blood across the floor towards Longarm's booted toes and asked quietly, *"Heya, why did you just kill Pashungo?"*

Longarm reached inside his coat for a fresh smoke as he answered. "I didn't kill Pashungo. That son of a bitch I just killed killed Pashungo, and lots of other folk. As you can see, he can't say much now. But let me introduce you to the Kiowa Kid, anyways."

He took out two cheroots and struck a light for those in the room who hadn't given up smoking, permanent, as he let what he'd said sink in.

It didn't. Big Bear accepted his cheroot politely enough, but said, "Hear me, Meneaska-Washtay. One of us has to be crazy, and I don't think it's me. The Kiowa Kid was a white boy, killed many days ago by bad Indians!"

"So much for descriptions on hastily writ wanted papers," Longarm said. "Anyone can see by his features in repose that he could have passed his fool self off as a white with Indian blood or an Indian with white blood, depending on his brag of the moment. His most recent role was fake Ute, of course, and he was the only really bad Indian in these parts."

"Wait," Big Bear said. "What about all the others killed and scalped by at least one Indian on the warpath?"

Longarm looked disgusted and asked, "What Indian on what warpath? The only Indians left in these parts are the ones on this reservation. Most of 'em had a good alibi for at least one of the so-called Indian uprisings we've enjoyed of late. Those who can't be accounted for at the time of a killing have a tolerable alibi anyway. For just outside the reservation line stands a homestead inhabited by two helpless white women, their livestock, and other temptations few moody braves would be likely to pass up. As I rode around the past few days I noticed other tempting easy targets and, no offense, but when you red folk go on the warpath you're seldom so selective!"

He saw the Crow was listening now, so he added, "Pay attention. For it's sort of complicated, and I don't want to repeat my fool self. Take my word for things as I go along and I'll tell you how I figured some of the details when it's time to."

Big Bear nodded, soberly sucking on his cheroot. So Longarm leaned back against the dead agent's desk and said, "Here goes. In the beginning there was the Kiowa Kid, riding for his ass with a posse breathing down his neck. He'd lit out on a heavy white-shod horse, so he was leaving considerable sign across a recently rained-on prairie. They'd have no doubt caught him, had his luck not changed. But meanwhile a sassy Lakota gal called Dancing Antelope was being wicked, too. She'd just stole a mess of goodies from the Strong Heart Society and was riding off to sell 'em to white folk when she met up with the Kiowa Kid on the lone prairie. You want to guess what happened then?"

The Crow shrugged and said, "The girl was never seen alive again. The Kiowa Kid was a known rapist and killer. Where do you think he hid her body afterwards?"

"That's easy," Longarm said. "After he'd had his wicked way with the poor wicked gal, he dressed her in the duds he'd been wearing. Then he scalped her long hair off, put her face down on a red-ant pile, and rode off aboard her Indian pony. He kept his hat, boots, guns, and the Indian weaponry he'd robbed her of, of course."

Big Bear coughed on smoke going down the wrong way and protested, "That's *really* crazy! Are you trying to tell me the body the posse found and buried as the Kiowa Kid was the body of an Indian *woman?*"

Longarm said, "Ain't trying. Saying. Wire from the undertaker in Middle Fork just confirmed my suspicion. I know it sounds dumb, but stop and consider. Who in thunder would have thought to pull down the pants of what looked to be a dead man? She'd been laying flat on her face and tits for a spell before they found her, and you know how flat on the bottom dead cats, coyotes, and such can get."

"But what about her *complexion?* They thought they were looking for a white outlaw. Were they blind?"

Longarm held out his own suntanned hand. "Not really. Most of us Meneaska who spend a lot of time on the open range burn at least as brown as an Indian gal. There was likely more than one old boy in that posse whose exposed hide was as brown as what they saw of Miss Dancing Antelope's. Naturally, it never occurred to anyone to rip the shirt off and see if the body was paler in other parts. Besides all that, don't forget the body they found was covered with red ants and starting to get rancid in the hot sun. Overripe dead folk turn all sorts of funny colors!"

The Crow made a wry face and cut in to say, "I see how the posse accepted the dead Indian girl for the Kiowa Kid. What happened after that? Surely he couldn't get far naked or wearing a woman's clothes!"

Longarm smiled thinly. "That's one part he couldn't play, I reckon. He likely rode off sort of bare-ass. But of course he grabbed odds and ends along the way, off clothes lines he passed after sundown and such, and rode into Middle Fork dressed White again, albeit looking like a saddle tramp in the misfitting duds he'd purloined."

Big Bear frowned and said, "There *was* a saddle tramp. But he was killed and scalped, too!"

"I sure wish you'd just hush and listen, old son," Longarm sighed. "There never was no saddle tramp. Pay attention, damn it!"

The Indian hunkered down to smoke in silence, staring

at the dead man in the doorway.

Longarm went on. "He still had guns and money, despite his looks. So he had no trouble finding a place to board in Middle Fork as he lay low in town, waiting for word his case was closed and it was safe for him to drift on, no longer quite so nervous. But then, just as he was likely starting to feel safe at last, *I* came up here from Denver to sniff about. It was a fool's errand. I still don't know why they sent me. But the Kiowa Kid didn't know how dumb Washington can be. He knew my reputation as a fair tracker, so he figured I hadn't bought the tale of his demise and that I was tracking him."

The Crow grunted. "That must have frightened him very much."

Longarm said, "It frightened him enough to want to read my mail. He had to kill that Western Union clerk when the clerk told him it was against company policy. He pored over the messages the dead clerk had on hand. He found nothing telling him whether I knew he was alive or not. But he also found a wire saying a Ute peace officer named Pashungo was due in any old time."

Big Bear said, "Wait. How could he have hoped to pass for a Ute if he was a Kiowa breed? I speak a few words of Ute. They were my people's enemies, too, in the Shining Times. When I greeted the man calling himself Pashungo in Ute, he answered me in Ute, fluently."

Longarm nodded. "Sure he did. Don't you Crow and your Lakota enemies speak the same lingo? Don't Cheyenne and Blackfoot both talk Algonquin?"

"Yes, but—"

"But me no buts and pay attention, Mahto-Tonka. Kiowa, Comanche, Shoshone, and Ute all speak the same or closely related lingo. I tested him, too. But neither you nor me is fluent enough in Ute to tell if a man has a Kiowa accent or not."

"I'll take your word for a Kiowa being able to pass for a Ute," the Crow agreed. "What happened after he intercepted the night letter about poor Pashungo?"

Longarm said, "He couldn't ambush the Ute before he got here. He couldn't stay in Middle Fork after killing the Western Union clerk and getting the local law on the prod and looking out for strangers with more diligence than usual. So he rode out to plot his next moves in the privacy of the prairie."

Longarm blew a thoughtful smoke ring before he went on. "What happened next is sort of fuzzy, since everyone involved is too dead to fill in the details for us. But it looks like the killer met up with a pair of poor cossacks who was scouting for any Triangle Crown beef the phony prince hadn't already sold off. The phony saddle tramp opened fire on said cossacks and dropped one right off. The other, winged or just plain scared, lit out with the Kiowa Kid chasing him. At some distance the second cossack got blown out of the saddle, too. The Kiowa Kid put an arrow in his back to make it look like an Indian killing, but he didn't bother to scalp and mutilate him, since it didn't matter who he was when he was found. He left the poor cuss for dead and rode back to swap duds with the one placed more conveniently closer to town."

Big Bear looked up. "Heya! The saddle tramp you found was the dead cossack!"

Longarm nodded. "You're learning. He arrowed and mutilated the poor Russian so his own mother wouldn't have known him. We can assume he was the blond one, Ilya, since the sneak had some blond hair left over at the undertaking parlor, if you recall."

Longarm let that sink in as he blew another smoke ring. "Meanwhile, I was having troubles of my own. I found the dead gent fixed up to look saddle tramp and then rode on out to get captured by them crazy foreigners. Another mean-

173

while, the cossack left for dead, and not really in much better shape, woke up long enough to call or catch his thoroughbred left grazing as useless by the Kiowa Kid. The poor Russian hauled his dying self aboard and lit out for the home spread at a dead run, sadly confused by the one or more bullets and that Lakota arrow in him. His dramatic arrival confused the timing of his taking said arrow considerable, and of course when his cossack pals went looking for the sidekick he'd been riding with, they found what they took to be a dead American saddle tramp."

He blew a plume of smoke in the direction of the dead man in the doorway and said, "He sure was a confusing rascal, wasn't he? Anyway, after dark he rode into Middle Fork dressed Russian, just in case anyone noticed him creeping into Miss Dorothy's. Someone did, giving Russia a worse name than it really might deserve."

The Crow nodded, but asked, "Why did he want to rape and murder the woman undertaker, Meneaska-Washtay?"

Longarm shrugged. "The rape was just a bad habit he had. His real motive was duds. He knew he'd never get far as a cossack with sort of Indian features. But he knew that, like most undertakers, Miss Dorothy was sure to have some decent clothes on hand in case a customer came in dressed informal or torn up. He changed to sensible duds, then he rode off along the railroad right-of-way scattering the dead cossack's duds to make it look like a mad Russian had hopped a freight while in the act of undressing on the fly. I never bought that part at all, but the sheriff did, so I reckon it was worth the effort."

Big Bear said, "We are getting closer to the time he must have met the real Pashungo, I hope."

Longarm nodded. "We are. Them details are fuzzy, too, with nobody left to fill us in on the exact details of the ambush. Suffice it to say that the Kiowa Kid met Pashungo

174

on the trail from the west, murdered him, and switched identities again. He could hardly hang on to the Strong Heart Society's old weaponry if he meant to join up with the law to chase his fool self. So he used the arrows and paint he had left to stage that fake attack on the sod house before dropping them by the body of Pashungo. Do I really have to explain why he left the real Pashungo naked and painted to look like a dead wild Indian that harmless nester might have winged?"

The Crow smote his own forehead with a horny palm. *"Heya!* I was wondering how a Great Basin Indian seemed to be tracking so much better than me on my own prairie!"

Longarm said, "I was, too. He knew all sorts of things about the lay of the land and current events for a gent who'd just got here. But, though I suspicioned him, I still wasn't sure. I knew, whatever he was, he couldn't pass for a Russian cossack in broad day. And, aside from the dead undertaking gal, we still had to account for that attack on Miss Pretty Blankets by a paler-faced gent dressed Russian."

Big Bear grinned. "Hear me. Pretty Blankets is a Berdachee!"

Longarm grinned back sheepishly and said, "I know that now. I'm surely glad I didn't find out the way that otherwise innocent cossack did! I don't reckon I'd have beat the poor critter up and spit all over its warning beads, but some gents ain't as understanding. So you can't really blame a poor foreigner for acting upset when he reached under a gal's skirt and wound up with a man."

The Crow laughed. "The Berdachee was foolish to flirt with anyone who didn't understand Plains Indian custom. I wish I had been there to see it. It must have been a very funny thing to watch!"

Longarm nodded and continued. "Once I figured the attack on Pretty Blankets was a red herring I only had a few more things to check before I could be sure. Coming back I coffeed at the same homestead and found the tempting victims there safe and sound. I still had three missing whites to account for, who'd last been seen alive in the company of recently calmed Lakota. But we know how that turned out, don't we?"

The Crow said, "We do, and I feel very foolish about that, too. I believed the trader's common-law woman when she told me they'd ridden south together. I scouted for sign on barren ground, even though I'd never really seen them leave!"

"Let's stick to one killer at a time," Longarm said. "I sent you and this dead bastard to arrest her for two reasons. I didn't want her trying to compromise the arresting officer with scandalous talk about the way she might have served him in the guest quarters lest he get hungry and go poking about in the cellar for preserves and such. I wanted to double-check by wire about the body in the Kiowa Kid's official grave as well. Once the undertaker in Middle Fork assured me they'd exhumed a she-male with Indian bone structure, I had all the nails I needed in his box. So when I told him he was under arrest, as you can see, he didn't seem to grasp the advantages of surrendering peaceable to the inevitable. He sure was a moody son of a bitch."

Big Bear got back to his feet as he said, "I would have killed him, too. Now I'd better see if I can find a mop. He's making a terrible mess on that floor."

"There's an even worse mess to clean up down in the cellar," Longarm said. "This sure has been a messy case from start to finish." He blew a thoughtful smoke ring and added, "The hell of it is, I ain't even sure it's finished yet."

Chapter 14

Longarm met a tolerable-looking brunette on the train back to Denver, but failed to get anywhere with her. He didn't get mad. It made the game more interesting when an occasional player said no.

He rolled into Denver a little after eleven A.M., stowed his gear at his hired digs across Cherry Creek, and reported in at the federal building to find his boss, Billy Vail, out to lunch. He gave the report he'd written on the train to Henry and went out again to eat as well.

He had a few schooners of needled beer while he was at it and got back to the office at what he considered the tolerably reasonable hour of three P.M. Henry sniffed and said the boss was not only back, but had been so for some time now, so Longarm went on in to see him.

Billy Vail tried not to smile as he looked up from behind his desk to ask, "What happened? Did you skip dessert?"

Longarm saw the marshal had his report and a telegram on the green blotter between them. He sat down and lit a smoke.

Vail said, "This wire from Middle Fork says they've rounded up all the left-over horses, so your report makes even more sense, now. But I'm glad no judge and jury will

177

have to puzzle over this complexicated flimflam. It was mighty considerate of you to save all the bother of a trial by gunning the rascal in cold blood, Longarm."

Longarm said, "There was nothing cold-blooded about it, Billy. I was mighty peeved with the son of a bitch and, besides, I gave him a chance to come peaceable."

"I'll bet. I read in this report what you writ about that undertaking gal. You damn near put the pencil through the paper as you writ it."

Longarm shrugged. "What's done is done. The case of the Kiowa Kid is closed. What about the princess and her butler boyfriend? Have the eloping lovers been picked up yet?"

Vail leaned back and smiled like a fat old cat digesting a canary. "We have the phony prince. You'll never guess where he get arrested this morning," he chuckled.

"I might not have, if you weren't sitting there like a gambling man with a full house, Billy," Longarm said. "I told the princess of the wonders of Denver. I'm surprised they were dumb enough to come here."

"It wasn't so dumb," Vail said. "They knew it was a big town, and that the routes east and west were likely to be staked. Anyway, Murphy and Guilfoyle arrested the fake prince at the Palace, recovered a mess of jewels and cash, and got a full confession. He's already on his way East to be turned over to the Russian authorities, the poor bastard."

"What about old Princess Tasha?"

"She was out shopping or something when they busted in on her lover. We got the hotel and the Union Depot staked. Doubt she'll be dumb enough to make for either, now."

Longarm blew a thoughtful smoke ring and said, "So do I. Tell me something, Billy. If we mean to turn her over to the Russians to stand trial in Russia, would I be compromised as the arresting officer if she was to say some mean things about me?"

Vail laughed incredulously. "Jesus, her too?"

Longarm just looked sheepish.

"I don't see how it can affect her trial in Russia, if they even give her one," Vail said. "But don't you have to find the sneaky gal afore you can arrest her, compromised or not?"

Longarm consulted his watch. "Yep. I'd better get cracking, too, lest the ladies' hairdressers all close before I can get to every one."

He rose and, since Vail didn't say not to, stalked out.

It was a big town with lots of places to consider. So it was sundown when Longarm at last appeared at the Taj Mahal Baths, identified himself to the nice-looking ash blonde running it, and told her why he'd come.

The steam bath lady said there was indeed a she-male customer with a funny accent back in the steam rooms at the moment, but added that said customer was a redhead, or at least had a henna rinse.

Longarm nodded and said, "I know, ma'am. They told me at the beauty shop down the street that they'd turned a blonde into a redhead, recent. The outlaw gal I'm looking for has a habit of taking steam baths when she's upset, and if she ain't upset right now, she ought to be. Her being a princess and this being about the fanciest steam bath establishment a day's ride from the Union Depot adds up. I'll know for sure when I see her, red-headed or not."

The ash blonde sighed. "I do so hope we can keep this out of the papers. Are you going in to arrest her now?" she asked.

Longarm shook his head. "That could really get us in the *Denver Post,* if I was to grab the wrong naked lady in a cloud of steam. I'll just wait right here, if you don't mind.

179

Sooner or later she has to come out."

So he did, and whoever was back there taking a steam bath sure liked a long one. He and the ash blonde got to talk for an hour or more and she even served him coffee and cake while they waited. They were just about getting to be old pals when the door leading to the steam rooms opened and Princess Natasha came out, dressed at last. She looked mighty surprised to see Longarm rising to his feet in the reception room. But she knew he knew her, despite the funny color of her still damp hair. So she ran over to him and bleated, "Oh, Custis, I'm so glad you found me first! Prince André is in town!"

Longarm snapped the cuffs on her as he said, "No, he ain't. He's on the eastbound for Washington. If we hurry, we can get you aboard the *next* one bound for there."

Tasha looked down in horror at the cuffed wrists he was holding by the linking chain. "You can't send me back to Russia! They'll kill me, Custis!" she sobbed.

"I know, and I'm mighty sorry about that, Princess," he said. "But you should have thought about that before you killed your husband. You might make it easier on yourself if you came clean about where he's buried and so on."

She spat like a cat and started calling him awful things in French and Russian. He nodded to the ash blonde, who'd been watching with wide-eyed interest, and said, "I sure thank you, ma'am. The coffee and cake was swell and the company was sweet, too. But I'd best take this spitting vixen over to the lockup, now."

The ash blonde opened the door for them. "I told you my name was Silvia," she said. "Did I mention I'd be getting off work in an hour or so?"

Longarm nodded soberly and said, "You surely did, Miss Silvia. And it won't take me no hour or so to turn this less friendly lady over to the matron at the federal detention house."

180

As he led, or sort of dragged, the moaning princess out, the ash blonde murmured, "Hurry back and you can help me close."

He said, "I mean to. But tell me something, Miss Silvia. If you're fixing to close up later this evening, does that mean the steam will be shut off by the time I get back?"

She shrugged and said, "There'll be some pressure in the pipes until midnight, I suppose. Why do you ask?"

"Just wondering, Miss Silvia. We'll talk about it later tonight."

Watch for

LONGARM AND THE STEER SWINDLERS

sixty-fifth novel in the bold
LONGARM series from Jove

coming in May!